SYDNEY SCOTT

EVERNIGHT PUBLISHING ®

www.evernightpublishing.com

PRACTICE MAKES PERFECT

Copyright© 2024

Sydney Scott

ISBN: 978-0-3695-1101-0

Cover Artist: Jay Aheer

Editor: CA Clauson

SYDNEY SCOTT

DEDICATION

To the person reading this book. Please know that you are enough.

SYDNEY SCOTT

PRACTICE MAKES PERFECT

Starlight Lake, 2

Sydney Scott

Copyright © 2024

Chapter One

Carter

The sight of moving boxes greets me as I stumble out from my bedroom in the apartment I share with my sister, her son, and her boyfriend. Not boyfriend, I correct myself, *fiancé,* and after today, I won't be sharing the apartment with anyone. Loneliness threatens just as it does every time I think about Maya and her small family are moving into our old childhood home, something that's been on the horizon ever since Jake bought it for her and subsequently proposed this past Valentine's Day. They've been staying here with me while some necessary renovations were under way, but those are all finished and now they're ready to move in and move on with their lives. If only I could be so lucky. While my sister is engaged to be married to the man of her dreams and the father of her almost three-year-old son, I'm about to be more alone than I have been in a long time.

Six years ago this November, we lost our parents in a drunk driving accident. Maya came home from college and immediately moved in with me after our childhood home was repossessed due to some financial blundering on our parents' part. Two years later, she got pregnant with JJ and for a while, it was the three of us against the world. We had a great routine going. Maya and JJ would hang inside the store we own, Hodgepodge, and liaise with customers and artisans while I spent most of my time out in the workshop, focusing my efforts on creating new furniture and other woodworking pieces that were requested of me. We'd have dinner together, and then enjoy each other's company until bedtime. To help Maya out, I also spent a good amount of time hanging out my nephew, taking him to the park or playing any number of games with him to help tire him out before I sang him to sleep for his nap or bedtime. It was nice to have those special moments with JJ, and helping to take care of him and my sister gave me a sense of purpose outside of work. Now that those days are over, I'm feeling slightly depressed about the whole situation.

It's not that I'm not happy for my sister. I am. The fact that Jake disappeared for three years and came back to her was incredible, a miracle really, and seeing Maya and JJ as happy as they have been these last few months fills my heart with so much joy and gratitude that it sometimes feels like I can't contain it all. My sister having everything she ever wanted is more than I could ever hope for, and now she does. We struggled for so long, her in particular, and now her romantic and financial worries are behind her. My worries are as present as ever, and now that I will be on my own, I'm actually a bit concerned for myself. Before I could channel all of my time and energy into my family, but now that's not the case, and I'm not sure what to do

It's not like I'm a recluse or anything, but I'm not exactly Mister Social either. Being around other people isn't something I dread, it's just that with the last few years being so busy with work to keep the store solvent and my helping Maya with her son, I haven't had a whole lot of time for friends or dating. The idea of having someone to love who would love me in return has been on my mind since I was younger, but between dealing with the grief of losing my parents and Maya getting pregnant two years later, dating didn't just get pushed to the back burner, it got taken off the stove and put on ice almost permanently.

Admittedly, finding that special someone could have been more of a priority for me if I really wanted it to, but it wasn't like I was having much luck before my parents' accident anyway. Starlight Lake is a small town and the dating pool is even smaller. It seems like every woman here has already gone on a date with me and declined a second, or hasn't been interested in dating me at all. Expanding my search area to other towns on the dating apps hasn't provided more options either, so eventually I stopped looking altogether.

Dating apps are all about snap judgments based on looks rather than based on who the person really is, and I understand that, but it doesn't make it suck any less for me. Attraction is important, and while I'm a decent looking guy, I'm not exactly the type of man you immediately swipe right for. My father, Stellan Johansen, on the other hand, came to the states from Norway and was basically a modern-day Viking with the face and body of a warrior. He was tall and broad shouldered, with flowing golden locks, a strong nose and jaw, icy blue eyes, and the kind of muscles I could only get from hours in the gym and an all grilled chicken and vegetable diet. He was the type of guy women would practically swoon over, batting their eyelashes at him every chance they got.

Maya inherited his striking Scandinavian looks and charming personality, whereas I take after my mother, Olive. She was a little quieter, a little more reserved when it came to her dealings with others, and she looked more like your average girl next door than Viking princess. Her hair was dark brown, her stature on the shorter side, and her body soft from a mixture of genetics, strong dislike of exercise, and deep love of sweets. My father believed her to be the most beautiful woman he had ever seen, and I agree that she was beautiful, it's just that most times I wish I had taken after Dad when it comes to my appearance.

At five feet eleven, I'm no slouch in the height department, and I have muscles built from long days of hard work in my shop, lifting and sculpting wood furniture for hours on end, but my face is a little rounder than I would like and my dark brown hair is wavy and never seems to want to settle in one spot. Running a hand over it now as I pad over to the kitchen and turn on the coffee maker confirms that once again, I have a massive case of tangled bed head. Maya tells me it's not my appearance, but my lack of confidence that is the cause of my dating woes. While I agree with her that my confidence could benefit from a little boost, it's hard not to think that my looks aren't a factor when I've lost track of the number of disappointed glances I've gotten from dates when we first meet in person.

Women on the apps read about my being a small

town woodworker and see the flannel I often wear, and they expect a lumberjack, an alpha male mountain man that can sweep them off their feet and that they'll fall instantly, madly in love with. You would think they would see that wasn't likely to be the case from my app photos, but they don't. Maybe they hope the reality is better than what's on screen, but when they show up and get a somewhat timid guy who would rather sculpt wood into something useful than spend hours sculpting his own body into one of a Greek God or perfect his lumberjack persona, it becomes obvious that I'm not what they were hoping for. That kind of fantasy is a lot to live up to, and it doesn't help when you're starting at a disadvantage of what it seems most women around my small town want.

With a sigh, I open the cabinet and take out three mugs and a new sippy cup for JJ. As the coffee percolates, I start making some breakfast for the family. My eyes flick over to the pile of cardboard boxes near the corner of the family room. We're going to need a good start if we're moving all of those today. At least it's June and there isn't a cloud in sight. Glancing out the window to see a clear sky brightens my mood slightly, and I'm grateful for it. Summer is my absolute favorite time of year. I may not be a lumberjack, but I know my way around the woods and enjoy hiking, camping, and going out on the lake, squeezing as much time out in nature as I can into the warmer months. At least I'll have those activities to look forward to when I'm dealing with the lonesomeness that's creeped its way into my heart over the years and seemed to set up shop permanently.

The door to the second bedroom creaks open, drawing my attention there just in time to watch JJ shoot out and run towards me in his footie pajamas while nearly slipping on the hardwood floor. "Carda," he squeals. He's still unable to enunciate my full name, but it's not like I mind. He can call me anything he wants in that sweet little voice. My nephew basically has me wrapped around his little pinky finger and he knows it. With a smile on his chubby face, he skids straight into my legs and holds them tight. A smile of my own spreads across my face at the familiar gesture as I lean down and pick him up.

"Hey there, little J," I cheer before blowing a raspberry on his soft cheek. The sound reverberates in the small kitchen space and it makes him giggle even harder. "What do you want for breakfast this morning?" It's the last time I'll be making him breakfast in this apartment, but I manage to hold my disappointment at that fact at bay and keep my expression bright for him. My nephew will still be around, and I can still do things for him, it will just be different. There is a mostly-finished project down in my workshop that will be an awesome treehouse bed for JJ when it's finished, so working on that will help keep my mind off of my family's absence as well.

"Pankies," he shouts and wiggles in my grasp. Putting him down, I watch as he starts pushing his little helper stool over to the counter and smacks the granite with his open palms. "Pankies, pankies!"

"All right, all right. Pancakes it is," I chuckle.

My hand reaches over to ruffle his auburn curls before I set him up with a bowl of sliced grapes to snack on while he waits. Normally, I would go for something much easier than pancakes, but it's a big day, and was specially requested, so I don't feel obligated to reel him in. As I start gathering up the necessary ingredients, I hear Maya's slippers shuffling across the floor as she comes into the kitchen and pecks her son on the cheek. When I spot her expression out of the corner of my eye, my heart swells. She looks incredibly happy, almost glowing with the emotion, and no matter how much I'm going to miss her and little J, it's nice to see her looking more rested, more refreshed, and more cared for than she has in quite some time.

"Morning, Mai," I say to her as I grab a large bowl.

"Good morning," she mutters around a large yawn. She starts pouring the coffee into the mugs I've laid out and I pass over the vanilla bean creamer I snagged from the fridge while I was grabbing eggs and milk for the pancakes. Our mealtime routines are like a well-rehearsed play at this point, another thing that will be changing come this time tomorrow. You'd think that I would be happy to be back to cooking for one, but it's been at least six years since that's been the case, and I'm not even sure I know how to do it anymore. That thought is more depressing than I would like it to be, and my hand comes up to my chest to rub at the ache that's formed there.

Maya peeks at me from the corner of her eye. "Ready to have this place all to yourself? No more JJ sneaking into your room to wake you up before you're ready. No more sharing a bathroom with three other people," my sister says, a hopeful grin on her face. She knows me better than anyone, so it's no surprise that she's trying to get me to see the good of this whole situation while I seem determined to only see the downside.

A rueful smile plays at my mouth as I mix up the batter for pancakes. "Well, I certainly won't miss the old 'sock on the door' system for letting me know you and Jake need some alone time," I tell her with a shudder. "I've learned more about your sex life over the last six months than I have ever wanted to know." It certainly didn't help that I wasn't getting any myself. Every time I came home to that little reminder to make myself scarce was another time I was reminded of how utterly hopeless my own personal life was.

Maya's cheeks darken in a blush as she adds creamer to the coffees and passes me my favorite mug. "Sorry about that," she replies. The little gleam in her eye tells me she's not as repentant about it as she's making out though. "You could have taken advantage of the system yourself, you know."

I scoff, whipping the batter harder than necessary. "That would require someone to actually want to go out on more than one date with me first." The words tumble out before I can draw them back, and I glance over at Maya just in time to see her frown. Great. Sibling lecture incoming in three … two…

"I don't like it when you talk about yourself like that," she admonishes. Her eyes flick over to JJ who is too busy smashing grapes all over the counter to notice either of us or what we're talking about. "It's not good for JJ to hear his uncle being so down on himself. Besides, it's been forever since you even tried to get a date, so how do you know there isn't someone out there just waiting for you to ask them out?"

With a sigh, I turn to her and clasp her shoulder. "I'm not trying to be down on myself and I'll watch what I say around JJ more closely." The promise is one I intend to keep, but I can't promise the self-conscious thoughts won't continue to swirl around in my mind, much like the blueberries in my pancake mixture. Turning back to the griddle, I distract myself by pouring some batter and enjoying the satisfying sizzle that hits my ear as it hits the surface. As I watch the batter start to bubble, I think a little more about what Maya's said. Maybe I have been too hard on myself as far as dating goes. Another shot at it wouldn't be such a bad idea, and it has been a long time. "You're right. It has been too long since I really put myself out there. Maybe I can use the free time I'll have now to remedy that."

"There you go," Maya says with a bright smile. "Any girl would be lucky to have you." She turns her attention back to JJ and starts to clean up his first attempt at winemaking when Jake emerges from their bedroom looking way more put together than anyone has a right to after just waking up. My hand reaches up in one last attempt to smooth out my own matted hair when I get a glimpse of his. Not a single red curl out of place, the jerk.

Jake nods a greeting to me as he joins Maya and JJ at the counter. "Good morning, beautiful," he tells my sister. His words proceed his leaning in for what I am sure will be a very passionate kiss, but I turn away in enough time to miss it. They're not shy about showing affection in front of me or JJ, but it feels wrong to witness something so intimate, especially when it causes a little sting of envy in me every time I do. That's the kind of happiness I want, I think to myself as I flip the pancakes.

The love my sister and her fiancé found is the type of love born from two people who fell for one another instantly, and while they had to deal with a period of absence and other obstacles on the way towards their happily ever after, they both seem to be stronger for it. Maya always describes the connection she feels with Jake as magical, as something that was written in the stars long ago that she had no hope of resisting. If I hadn't witnessed their coming back together for myself, I'm not sure I would have believed it, but I do, at least for the two of them. With both my parents and now Maya experiencing the 'love at first sight' phenomena, one could think I was hoping for the same thing myself, but that isn't the case.

While I've felt a slight inkling of that once in my life, I dismissed it as a fluke or wishful thinking on my part. There was no way a woman as stunning and dynamic as Jake's best friend Billie would have been interested in me anyway, no matter how much she likes to flirt with and tease me. That's just her personality and has nothing to do with her actually wanting me. As we all sit down to breakfast and the thought of having nights and weekends to myself stretches before me, the decision to try and find someone to spend my time with is an easy one. What I want is someone who appreciates me for who I am underneath the surface, who can see past the wild, wavy hair and soft features to see the caring, thoughtful, kind man I try every day to be. Now all I need to do is find the woman willing to do just that.

Chapter Two

Billie

Gray clouds threaten rain and there is hardly a single token of summer to be seen from the window of my office on the thirty-fourth floor of Mile High Consulting. At this moment, the Denver skyline isn't exactly awe inspiring, and the streets below offer nothing but a view of tiny people going about their business and cars passing over the dusty asphalt of downtown. I feel like a giant peering into a microscope, but nothing I see is entertaining me in the least. The whole scene mirrors my mood—dreary. It's been this way for the last eight months, not that anyone would be able to tell you that. Sharing feelings, at least, feelings that are anything other than happy or cheerful, isn't something I really do. "Billie is such a happy child," people would tell my mother and father. It was true then, and I would still generally consider myself to be a happy person most of the time. I have my parents to thank for that.

Ola and Ivan Kochev were transplants from Bulgaria, having moved to the United States in their early twenties. My father came from money back in the old country, and he invested it wisely upon his arrival, eventually partnering with my best friend Jake's dad and starting Mile High Consulting. The business grew successfully, and once it was established, I came along. My parents always spoke about their upbringing as being quite harsh with a lot of rules and regulations, and they wanted something different for me.

My mom stayed at home when I was a baby and raised me "free range," as she likes to call it. There were no strict routines or schedules to follow like there were for Jake. As soon as I was old enough to cross the street by myself, I was able to go where I wanted and do as I pleased as long as I was being safe and was home for dinner every night. It was a pretty sweet deal, one that allowed me to explore the surrounding neighborhoods and make friends all over that I could visit any time I liked. It was absolutely idyllic.

As I grew older, the good times kept rolling all throughout high school and college. "Life of the party," "social butterfly," and "good-time girl" were all words used to describe me during that time of my life. They still are, but it didn't bother me back then like it does now. Years ago, I actually enjoyed being the center of attention. Going out to house parties and later on to bars and nightclubs was my bread and butter. Being around others and having them enjoy my company made me feel good about myself, and I really liked having so many people I could count as friends. It was great ... until it wasn't. The older I got and the more I examined the relationships I had, the more I came to realize how little those "friends" actually cared about me beyond getting into the hottest spots, getting free drinks, and partying for a few hours before we'd part ways, never knowing anything more about one another beyond names and alcohol preferences.

At first, I was just as guilty. My role had been main party goer and queen bee of the club kids for such a long time that I had never really stopped to think about how little I knew about the people I was spending time with, or how little they knew about me. My senior year of college was when it finally hit me. A group of us had decided to road trip to Daytona Beach for Spring Break. It was cliché, but we figured it was our final year at the University of Florida, so why the hell not? About one hour into the trip, after we had exhausted all talk of which clubs to hit and what beaches would have the best parties, an awkward silence came over the car as we realized that beyond going out together, we really didn't know much about each other.

Deciding that it was time to change all that, I started to chat everyone up about their favorite movies, but it quickly devolved into whether or not I knew any movie stars. After reminding everyone that I was from Denver, not Hollywood, and didn't know any, the car fell silent again and everyone turned to their phones with no one else even attempting any kind of conversation. The people I had been spending most of my time with didn't even remember where I was from, and in all fairness, I couldn't remember their hometowns either. It was a sobering realization, one I wish I had come to years earlier.

Looking back now, I realize those friendships were just surface level, and that's perfectly fine if that's what you're looking for, but by the time I turned twenty-three, I was wanting more than that. Jake was in Washington, and while we kept in touch and remained as close as two people can when separated by great distance, it wasn't enough. Wanting to change that, I tried to expand my horizons a little, making time to read more books, going to cinema I might not normally watch all in an attempt to really explore who I was underneath the facade I had inadvertently constructed for myself. I made attempts to get to know people better, or even get to know new people, but my reputation at school had already been cemented as one of a "party girl," so all anyone ever wanted to hear from me was where the next get together was or which shoes were best for dancing at the local nightclub. Graduation was a blessing and I looked forward to the change of moving back to Denver, but that didn't last long either.

It was supposed to be different here. A job was always waiting for me at my dad's business consulting firm, and with a major like tourism management, I shouldn't have been surprised that I was placed in the client relations department. At first it was just making sure prospective clients were happy when they came in for meetings. Fetching coffee and making sure catering orders were placed was the bulk of my work for the first year and half of my career, and I didn't mind it in the least. Slowly, it evolved into more. Taking clients out to lunch, dinner, and even classy nightclubs or high-end bars when the occasion called for it became the norm for me and it was like I was back in college all over again.

Sliding back into the role of "party girl" was so easy, like putting on a second skin that was comfortable and familiar while being restrictive at the same time. If all I had to concern myself with was whether or not the client was having a good time, I didn't have to be anything more than a pretty face with a joke or two to keep the atmosphere light and fun. After so many years of pretending to be nothing more than that, though, I'm starting to wonder if maybe I'm not really pretending after all. Maybe I am nothing more than my appearance.

The men I used to date would say that's the case, if they stuck around long enough to tell anyone, anyway. My relationships, if you can even call them that, have all been with men who are a lot like the persona I project out into the world. They're looking for a good time and can't be bothered with anything too serious, anything that would require more of them than wearing the right clothes, surrounding themselves with the right people, and flashing a straight-toothed smile for any camera that happens to point their way. It definitely wasn't romantically or personally fulfilling, but for a long time that didn't matter. Jake eventually moved back to Denver, and his friendship and our interactions filled my bucket enough that the lack of substance in my dating life didn't matter, but one friend can only do so much.

Eventually, I got tired of the surface level relationships and moved on to keeping it simple with the occasional hook-up, but I don't even bother with those anymore. What would be the point? I'm not getting what I need from the relationship and there are plenty of toys in my nightstand drawer to scratch the itch when I needed. A warm body would be nice, but that would require I put myself out there in a way I'm not sure I'm ready for. Finding out there isn't more to me than what's on the surface isn't something I'm certain I could handle right now. Jake tells me that I don't give myself enough credit for being a good person, and I should believe my best friend. He knows me better than anyone else, but I've kept things even from him. How I really feel about myself deep down is a secret I've kept from everyone, so how much can I really trust his judgment?

My cell phone rings and I spin around in my large office chair to grab it from my desk, smiling brightly when I see my friend's name flashing across the dark screen. It's great to hear from Jake and his call also provides a welcome distraction from my intrusive thoughts. "I was just thinking about you," I confess, mustering up as much cheer as I can. Talking to Jake is both a pleasure and a pain. Talking to him and hearing all about his life in Starlight Lake is lovely, but the ache of loneliness is always closer to the surface when he calls, a reminder that he's not here and that I'm all alone.

A low chuckle comes across the line and I smile at the sound. "Is that a good thing, or should I be worried that you're plotting something?"

I scoff. "You say plotting as if you don't always end up having a good time whenever we get together."

Jake may be more of a homebody than I am, but he's always a good sport and comes along when I ask him to. "Besides, I don't have time to plot anything. I'm up to my ears in work," I lie. Gazing around my mostly empty desk tells a very different story. Keeping other people entertained doesn't require much paperwork and most of my job takes place outside of the office anyway, but I don't want him to worry about me. When he moved, Jake pulled me aside and asked multiple times if I would be okay. Despite knowing the opposite, I assured him I would be. It wasn't as if I could beg him to stay and move his family here so that I wouldn't feel deserted. People may think I'm that selfish, but I would never do that.

Jake hums, not buying my bullshit for one minute. He worked here, so it's not like he doesn't know that I normally roll into the office around 10:00, coordinate a few events for clients and then get ready to head out to whatever bar, club, or sporting event I'm showcasing for the same people over and over again. Luckily, he won't call me out on my little fib. "Glad to hear things are going well. I just called to let you know that we have set a date for the wedding. It's November 12th, so mark that on your calendar. Oh, and we're officially all moved into the house and you are welcome to be our first guest anytime you want."

"Really?" My voice going higher than normal exposes just how much hope is laced in it. A visit sounds like just what I need, but I don't want to sound too desperate. Clearing my throat, I try to go for a much cooler response. "I mean, that's great, but I'll have to check my schedule of course."

"Oh, for sure. We wouldn't want to pull you away from any big plans you might have. I know you're probably booked up with your other friends for at least the next month." There's no mocking in his tone because Jake believes what everyone else does, that I have a mountain of friends to call upon whenever I want when the reality is that the nights I'm not working are spent alone in front of the television as I watch the latest season of whatever trashy dating show happens to be on.

"How is the new place anyway?" The question is my desperate attempt to think about anything but my sad life and how I'm too afraid to do anything to try and fix it. It's ironic that someone most people would describe as fearless isn't any braver than your average bunny rabbit.

Jake sighs happily and I can picture the sappy smile on his face as he thinks about how amazing his life has turned out. Almost four years ago, Jake fell in love at first sight with a woman named Maya and had a one night stand, only to come back to Denver for three years in a futile attempt to live the life he was "supposed to." When he returned to Starlight Lake three years later, he learned that not only was Maya still there and still as equally in love with him as he was with her, but he also had a little boy named JJ. The kid is basically a carbon copy of his dad in every way, except for of course his reluctance to be my new bestie. It took a lot of visits, and a lot of money spent on presents, but I think JJ is finally warming up to me.

"It's fantastic, Billie. Maya is so delighted to be back in her childhood home, and there's a kind of peace about her that wasn't there before. I think it's helped give her a little bit of closure about losing her parents."

My stomach hurts at even the most fleeting thought of losing one of my parents, so I can't even begin to imagine what Maya and her brother had to deal with over the last six years. "Well, I'm glad Maya is liking it, and you know what they say, happy almost wife, happy life," I tell him, trying to disguise my sadness with a joke.

Jake and Maya getting engaged was fantastic news, but it did make me the teeniest bit jealous that while my friend is racing from one major life milestone to the next—kid, fiancé, home ownership—I'm nearly thirty years old and feel as if I've barely left the starting blocks.

Fortunately, Jake doesn't pick up on my cheerlessness and chuckles at my joke. "It is a happy life," he admits. Hearing his giddy tone has me making a more concerted effort to stow the slight bitterness I feel and just be happy for my friend. "JJ is loving having so much space to run around and having his own room too. I think it helps that Carter built him a bed that doubles as a play fort, so it's like having a bedroom and playroom all in one."

The mention of Maya's brother Carter cheers me slightly, and my eyes flick to my computer where I am tempted to navigate to Hodgepodge's social media site to see if there are any new pictures of him. Doubtful since I just checked this morning, but you never know. While I can resist the urge to check the website, I can't help but ask about my favorite woodworker. "How is Carter by the way? Still pining away for me?" It comes across like a joke, but I honestly wouldn't mind if someone like him were pining for me. Someone who is responsible and has it all together would be a nice change of pace as far as dates go.

Last November, when I hauled Jake back to Starlight Lake to end his misery and see Maya again, in addition to the surprise of finding out Jake had a son, I was also surprised to see that son had a sexy uncle. Carter is nothing like the men I have dated in the past. His good looks aren't at all obvious, but instead he is incredibly attractive in an unassuming, boy-next-door kind of way. His hair is always tousled, not from a half hour of meticulous styling with a mountain of expensive products, but from simply running his strong, capable hands through it. His moss green eyes are soulful and bright at the same time, like he can see beneath the surface of who I am and likes what he's found. He had a nice physique too, if you know to look for it. Underneath the ill-fitting jeans and loose flannel shirts lies a stack of lean muscles and pert ass. I wouldn't mind sinking my teeth into. The man doesn't know how to dress for his size, but I would happily strip him down and teach him a thing or two about his body before clothing it properly.

Despite only having spent a handful of hours together, Carter is also easily one of the best people I have ever met. Most of what I know about him is second-hand, but it's all been nothing but good. *Carter made a rocking horse for JJ, Carter added some built in bookcases and refinished the floors in our new house for Maya. Carter helped me pick out the ring I proposed with.* The man is so selfless that I almost worry that he doesn't do anything for himself. If he let me, I would take care of him in any way he asked me to without complaint.

Anytime we are in the same space, I tell him as much, commenting on how hot he is and how he should show himself off more, but he doesn't seem to believe me. Some of it is teasing and flirting, but when I really consider my feelings, every word I say has more than a bit of truth to it. It's doubtful that a guy as thoughtful, talented, and dependable as he is would go for someone like me anyway, but that doesn't mean I can't internet stalk him a little and order pieces of his furniture for my apartment, purely to help him and his sister financially of course.

"I don't know if I would call it pining, though I appreciate the wood pun," Jake huffs. His words break into my thoughts about a certain flannel wearing mountain man, and I frown at the intrusion. "More like, he complained about your comments on the store's site, and is seriously considering blocking you again."

I stifle a snort because my comments are a little over the top. "It's not like I'm sliding into his DMs and asking him to send me nudes or anything," I say with mock outrage. Doing just that is something I have almost considered during the long hours of particularly lonely nights, but luckily for us all, I do have a modicum of restraint.

"*Yet*," Jake adds with a sigh. "Just … do me a favor and leave him alone for a while. I think that us moving out has him feeling a little down."

My brow furrows with concern. He's never been chipper exactly, but I still don't like thinking of Carter as feeling poorly. My chest feels tight at the thought of my hard-working wood maker being anything less than his normal, reservedly happy self. My hand finds its way to the space above my heart, resting there lightly to try and ease the ache. "Fine," I exhale. "I'll keep my online harassment to a minimum."

"Thank you," Jake says with more relief than I feel is warranted. My commenting is meant to be a confidence boost, but I don't want to add stress to Carter's life. It's not like anything could ever happen between us anyway. For one, he's up in the mountains while I'm here in the city. Secondly, we're much too different. He's a serious and responsible individual, and I'm good for fashion advice, a night at the club, and not much else. "I better get going. We still on for dinner when I come into town next month?"

"Sounds good," I reply automatically. My thoughts are still stuck on my friend's soon-to-be brother-in-law. "Talk to you later."

"Bye, Billie," Jake says. The end of the call brings my attention back to my office, my eyes roaming from my nearly empty desk to the stark gray walls and sparse shelves. The room is devoid of any artwork, knickknacks, or personal photos. Personal photos would require I have people to hang out with that are worthy of memorializing, and while I have a picture frame of me and Jake with our parents on the corner of my desk and one of him with Maya and JJ, no one else has made the cut.

A knock sounds at my door and my eyes roam over to my assistant, Cheryl. She's the fifth assistant I've had this year and I have no hope for her lasting any longer than the others. It's not them or me that's the problem, but dealing with the constant influx of requests from clients and other people about where to go and what to do that drives them to quit. People around the office call my phone the "party line," and they're not far off. "Billie. The reps from the Sanderson Group called and wanted to know where you'll meet them for dinner," she says, adjusting her dark framed glasses. "Oh, and Tom Renfrey is on the line and wants to know if you could recommend a good wine bar for him to be photographed at."

"Tom…?" I ask. Flipping through my mental Rolodex and coming up blank, I look over at my assistant for guidance on who the hell she is talking about. There are far too many people calling for this kind of information to be able to keep track of, but it would be bad for business for me to turn any of them down.

"Renfrey. You took him and another client out last month and he thought you might know the best place to go." She looks about as tired as I feel, and it isn't even 1:00 in the afternoon.

"Thanks, Cheryl. You can put him through," I tell her. Plastering a fake smile on my face and trying to psych myself up for another conversation about wine bars and other nightlife activities that ultimately mean nothing to me anymore, I prepare to answer the call. It seems like all I do lately is fake it. I want to be more than the person you go to for a good time, but as I pick up the phone with false cheer in my voice, I fear that will probably never happen.

Chapter Three

Carter

Hodgepodge is quiet this afternoon. Too quiet. What I wouldn't give for a customer rush right now to save me from my overthinking about how long the last few weeks have felt. Ever since Maya, Jake, and JJ moved out, it's like time has started to drag from one dull moment to the next. My eyes roam around the shop and take in the various artisan pieces on display in a futile attempt to take my mind off my troubles. Pressed flower and white clay dishes stand out against the dark gray walls and I make a mental note to compliment Mrs. Hamstead, the creator of the pieces, the next time I see her.

Maybe I could hang out with some of the other local artisans to fill my abundance of free time. Maya extended a nightly dinner invitation to me before she moved out, but I can't keep imposing upon her or her family to fill my loneliness. Once a week is enough. Besides, spending time in my childhood home still feels a bit odd. It's the same house, but it feels very different, and it's not the renovations that were done. It's still strange to think of it as Maya's house, and difficult to stay there without seeing ghosts of the past around every corner. Maybe I would feel differently if I had more of a future ahead of me, but I don't.

My hand reaches down and picks at the frayed edge of my flannel shirt, the same flannel that belonged to my father. To some it might seem silly, especially since they are about a size too large for my frame, but wearing my dad's shirts helps me feel closer to him. The man was a force of nature, shooting a smile over to anyone who looked his way and possessing an unmatched patience for those who wanted to bend his ear about his furniture, his Norwegian upbringing, or even something as mundane as the weather. Dad was larger than life in more ways than one, his personality shining through no matter what the occasion or his mood. That kind of presence isn't something I think I'll ever be able to live up to. Still, I like to think that he would be proud of me for carrying on with the business at least.

My gaze flicks to the wall where a wooden valknut hangs. It was one of the first pieces of décor my father created and added to the store once it was passed onto him and my mother by my grandfather. Staring at the three interlocking triangles that represent "family" has me wondering if my parents, and my father in particular, would be as pleased with my current single status as they would about the business. "Family first," was my dad's motto, and for a while I forgot about that. My parents' death hit me pretty hard. Losing that kind of support and influence so suddenly was jarring to say the least, and for those first two years I kind of sunk into my grief. Working, eating, and trying to sleep were really the only things on my daily to-do list, but once Maya found out she was pregnant, I had to push through the pain of that loss and step up, once again embracing my father's motto.

Maya tells me I did a good job, helping her when she was a single mom and being an attentive uncle to JJ, but I wonder if maybe I shouldn't have been thinking a bit more selfishly at times. I could have been there for my sister and nephew while also trying to take steps towards creating a family of my own. Of course, that would require putting myself out there and I'm still not sure that's something I can do just yet. The desire is there, but my past experiences keep holding me back.

It's been six years since my last date, and eight

since the last time I had sex with another person. Hook-ups aren't something I can do as it's always been difficult for me to be with someone intimately without getting to know them better first. I had a girlfriend, Betty, in high school, but we were both always so busy that we did little more than hang out on occasion. We kissed and made-out, but we never came close to having sex, and when she moved after graduation, things naturally ended. After her, there was someone from my high school choir class that I reconnected with when she moved back home after graduating from college. We were decent friends in high school and fell back into a relationship easily enough, but it still took a good two months of dating before I felt connected to Jill enough to have sex. We broke up a few months later when she decided to move to Michigan for graduate school, but I doubt we would have lasted much longer anyway.

Our relationship was more platonic than romantic, neither of us really seeming to experience sparks of attraction when we were together. Since then, I've had a few first dates, but nothing more than that. I need to feel confident that the other person really cares about me before I can open myself up sexually, and most women aren't willing to stick around that long, especially when you already aren't living up to their expectations in other ways like looks or social ability. The one time I did feel that instant attraction was with Billie, and I wrote it off as a natural reaction to such a stunning woman. The moment I laid eyes on her my whole body felt flushed with a fever and I couldn't take my eyes off her. When she smiled, it was like the fire spread to my heart and opened it up to a whole new world of possibilities. Before I had a chance to process any of that, Maya and I were whisking JJ home so she could deal with Jake's reappearance, and that was that.

The shop bell chiming saves me from my pondering the strange occurrence with Billie any further and draws my attention to the front of the store. A well-dressed woman with strawberry blonde hair strolls in. She is conventionally attractive, but still, I don't feel much beyond an appreciation for the aesthetic appeal of her symmetric features. "Good morning," she calls out. Her melodic voice hits me first as she breezes towards the counter. "I have an order for pick-up. It's under the name Montgomery."

"Of course," I tell her. Recognizing the name from the dual spiral stools I created just last week, I give her a friendly smile and verify her payment in the computer. "It looks like you're all settled up and I have the finished product ready to go. I'll be back in a minute." Striding over to the back room, I grab a stool with each hand and carry them out to the front for inspection. "Here we are. Everything to your liking?"

Her eyes take a perusal over the stools. "Looks great. I love your work," she gushes, smiling widely and batting her eyelashes at me. Maybe some stray saw dust came up from the stools or something. "Do you ever give private lessons?"

My brow furrows. "No, never. There are too many safety and liability issues for that," I explain. Safety has always been a big concern for me, more so since we lost our parents. Logically, I know that a drunk driver has little to do with what goes on in my workshop, but it was a good reminder that one stupid mistake can have lasting consequences. "I think the town has workshops available if you're really interested."

The woman smiles, but looks disappointed. "Thanks. I'll look into that, but if you change your mind, I'll be around." She grabs both of her stools and exits the shop, seeming a bit less excited about her purchase than she had moments ago.

"Oof. That was brutal." I turn to see my sister holding my nephew in her arms as she leans against the side of the office door. "You do realize she was flirting with you, right?"

I scoff, crossing my arms over my chest. "I highly doubt that," I tell my sister. My cheeks pull into a smile as I gaze over at my nephew who has the sleepy eyes of a toddler recently woken from his nap. My hand automatically reaches over to ruffle his curls and I'm rewarded with a giggle from JJ.

"Carter," my sister sighs. She puts JJ down at the small play table we have set up for him in the office and pats his back. "You're never going to meet someone if you don't open yourself up to opportunities like the one you just had. She was pretty, seemed friendly. What was the problem?"

My shoulder bobs up and down quickly as I stare down at my feet. "I don't know. She was fine, I guess." My head knows that the woman was more than fine in almost anyone else's eyes, but I need more than that. I *want* more than that. After waiting this long, I want the sparks of attraction as well as an ease of conversation, and while I know I need to take the first step in order to get to know someone better, it's hard after so long of being out of the dating game. "It's been a long time, Mai. I'm not comfortable in social situations, and beyond that, I'm not really sure how to go about dating exactly anyway. I hate the apps."

Maya comes over and rubs my back lightly. "I'm know and I'm sorry. It sucks that it's basically get on an app or cross your fingers and hope you literally run into your soulmate, but you never know," she tells me. Her expression is hopeful and her piercing blue eyes shine brightly, but I don't share her optimism. "Maybe you'll find someone like I did."

My eyes roll up to the ceiling and I huff out a breath. "Still trying to get me to make a wish in the fountain?" I ask, shaking my head. "Never going to happen." What I won't tell her is that the last time we went to the holiday lighting festival with our parents, I did make a wish to find my special someone. When my parents were killed the following morning, I kind of stopped believing in magic of any kind. Just because it happened for Maya doesn't mean it will happen for me, and it's been almost six years. If my special someone isn't here already, I don't think she ever will be.

Maya looks slightly disappointed in my declaration, but she leaves it for the time being. "Suit yourself," she says with a knowing smile and walks back into the office. "More magic for me."

"As if you need any more," I call over to her, but she's already busy playing with her son. Now that she's back from lunch, I can get back to what I really enjoy doing. "I'm heading back to the workshop." Maya simply waves at me over her shoulder to shoo me away.

Through the store, out the back door, and across a short parking lot is all the space that separates my workspace from the selling floor. The smell of sawdust and pinewood fills my nose as I open the door and walk inside, taking stock of what projects are in a half-finished state and which are ready to ship. After grabbing my leather apron and tying it on, I walk over to my workbench, gliding my hands over the smooth surface of the wooden vases I've been working on today. After another round of sanding, I'll stain them a beautiful golden pecan color and send them off to the mysterious owner of Post Office Box 153 in Denver, the same person who has custom ordered at least half a dozen items over the last few months.

PRACTICE MAKES PERFECT

The orders come through the online store and are paid for by an account with a third party payment platform, so I have no idea who this person is. It ultimately doesn't matter, money is money after all, but it would be nice to know who is ordering such interesting items. The set of three wooden vases isn't unusual in itself, but together with the other items ordered, they stand out in a way that has me intrigued. Most of my orders are for furniture—stools, chairs, dining tables, and the like—but not PO Box 153. Whoever this person is has ordered a set of drink goblets, a fruit bowl, a honeypot and dipper, four small perfume bottles, a cigar box, and a pipe with a lion carved at the end. That last order especially had me brushing up on my whittling skills, but the customer was happy in the end and left a rave review on our site, so I guess I did all right.

My phone chimes, and after brushing the bits of sawdust that have already collected on my hand onto my jeans, I snag it from my pocket and smile when I see that the store's Instagram page has a new notification. Maya posts pictures on the site, most of which are different items that are available at the store. Occasionally, she'll get a picture of me in there standing next to one of my creations, just like she did this morning with the two stools I handed off moments ago. Sliding open my phone and navigating over to the social media app, I click it open, ready to read a comment from Jake's friend, Billie.

Billie is always the first to comment with something flirty or borderline inappropriate, and while I know she's just teasing me, each word she writes brings a smile to my face. Mostly. Sometimes they're a reminder of what I wish I could have but don't. A year ago when her comments started popping up, I blocked her before I knew who she was and that she wasn't being malicious. Now it's the only bit of contact I get from the gorgeous woman, so I cherish every like and comment, hoarding them like a dragon with his gold.

The smile I was sporting slides off my face when I see that it's just a like from our Aunt Sue. Sue was best friends with our mom and comes into town every now and then to visit, but we mostly keep in touch via text and social media comments. A notification from her comment pops up. "Keep up the good work, Carter," she writes. The praise feels good, but not as good as Billie's requests for me to post thirst traps or commenting that I'm looking particularly good that day. She has the uncanny ability to get my chest puffing out with pride in my appearance.

My thumbs scroll through past posts until I find one of her older comments. "The chair looks amazing, but not as amazing as the man that created it." Even if there is no truth in her words, my heart still swells slightly as I read them and the fire emojis she has trailing at the end. Clicking on her account name, billie@theparty, I navigate to her page and scroll though the pictures like I have many times before. Fortunately, it's public. Even if I had my own personal account, which I don't, I could never be brave enough to follow her.

My eyes move across the images that paint the picture of a very happy, very social woman. She's constantly surrounded by other members of the beautiful people club, smiling, laughing, and generally looking like she is winning at life. The most recent picture is of Billie at some kind of high-end pub. She looks stunning. Locks of mocha brown hair cascade down past her shoulders in waves, and a bright, cheeky smile is on her face as she looks into the camera. She's wearing a professional looking black suit, but the jacket is open and shows off the lace corset underneath. God, even in her work clothes she looks like sin, the kind of sin men like me would happily burn in Hell for having committed.

PRACTICE MAKES PERFECT

Seeing the movie star handsome man standing next to her with his arm slung around her shoulders has jealousy slicing through my chest, but it has no right to be there. Billie isn't mine, nor will she ever be. Just because she's the one person I felt instantly attracted to and connected with doesn't mean anything. It was just a fluke, too much talk of magic in the air connected to Maya and Jake that night in November is what caused the sparks I felt shooting up and down my spine, not anything real. Granted, that fluke tends to repeat itself every time she comes to visit, but maybe I'm just projecting my desire for another person onto her. We don't know each other very well, and we most likely won't anytime soon.

With a sigh, I shove my phone back in my pocket and try to get back to work, but as I start sanding the vases, my mind can't help but wander back to Billie and her recent lack of activity on the store's page. Maybe she finally realized what most other women do halfway through a single date. I'm not really worth the time.

Chapter Four

Billie

The incessant ringing of my cell phone stirs me from a deep sleep. With a groan, I roll over and look at the clock on my nightstand. My eyes blink a few times against the bright light of morning as it pours in through the crack in my curtains, and I shake my head for a moment before peeking back at the clock, hoping the time I'm reading isn't correct. 6:00 in the morning is not an hour I am used to seeing, at least from this side of it. Plenty of all-night study sessions as well as never-ending partying kept me up until this hour, but even that ended years ago. Scrubbing a hand down my face, I reach over to my phone, immediately alarmed when I see that it's my father calling. He wouldn't call this early if it wasn't important.

"What's going on, Dad?" I ask in fluent Bulgarian. Both of my parents may have immigrated to the US long ago and speak perfect English, but outside of work we speak in their native tongue.

A heavy sigh pours over the speaker and I brace myself for some bad news. As far as I know, both of my parents are in good health. My father is a regular down at the boxing club and my mother goes on long walks or hikes with her friends daily, so I can't imagine that one or both of them is experiencing a health crisis. "This is a conversation better suited to the office, Biliyana," he says with a resigned tone.

My dad always calls me by my full name whether I am in trouble or not, so that doesn't give me any clue, but the fact that he wants to speak at the office is a little unusual. "Why at the office? Can't you tell me now?"

"No." It's a simple and direct reply, his tone

letting me know my presence is not a polite request. My parents weren't strict with me growing up, but they did earn my respect and no matter what, when one of them makes a demand, I go with it. "Come in as soon as possible. This cannot wait."

The lack of cheer in his voice has my stomach bottoming out. "Okay. I'll see you soon. Bye, Dad," I tell him. My father is almost always in a good mood when we talk to one another, so to say I am shaken is an understatement. Hopefully nothing is majorly wrong with the business since I know how important it is to him. Work is basically his number one activity and if he doesn't have that, I would start to worry about his health and happiness.

"Goodbye." With that final word from Dad, the rock that has formed in my gut settles in for the long haul. His tone was so serious and his words so frank that I'm freaking out a little bit.

My mind whirs with ideas of what could possibly be going on as I slide off my plush bed and pad over the carpet to my bathroom. The marble tiles feel cold against my bare feet and I shiver as I turn on the water in the large glass shower. The apartment is a luxury one, leased by the firm. Normally that kind of thing is reserved for executives only, but being the daughter of the owner comes with more than a few perks. Covering rent is still my responsibility, though it is discounted, another perk of being Ivan Kochev's daughter. Between that and my car being paid off, I'm able to invest most of my money in stocks and other things. My eyes flick over to the two wooden perfume bottles I ordered from Hodgepodge earlier this year and I smile. That is definitely an investment worth making. The other set were given to my mother who was brought to tears by the reminder of something her mother had when she was younger.

Between those and the other things I've ordered both for myself and my parents, I've probably kept Carter pretty busy.

My smile widens at the thought as I step into the warm water, letting it release a little bit of the tension that's settled into my body after my father's phone call. Picturing Carter in his workshop, the sinewy muscles of his forearms on display as he carves into a piece of wood has me wanting to linger in the shower for a bit and take care of another kind of tension, but I don't have time to indulge in that particular fantasy at the moment. After turning the water to cold and quickly washing up, I dry off and head over to my closet, trying to decide which outfit best works for a meeting of undetermined significance. Finally, I decide on a high-waist black skirt and pink blouse. Normally my style leans more toward sexy day-to-night ensembles, but if the business is in trouble, I need to look as professional as possible. After dressing quickly, I throw my wet hair into a high bun and make my way out to the kitchen.

My feet take me past the family room, the beige walls screaming for a bit of color. One of these days I'm going to replace all the black and white stock artwork with something more vibrant, more eclectic. Maybe another Carter Johansen original, I think to myself as I open the fridge and pull out some overnight oats. While I scarf down the blueberry flavored grains, the temptation to check on Hodgepodge's Instagram page is *real*. My fingers twitch with the desire to whip out my phone and take a gander at any new photos. It's been so hard not posting comments on the pictures I have seen, but I've persevered. As tough as it's been, thinking that I've been making Carter uncomfortable isn't something I can live with. Teasing and flirting is only fun if the attention is wanted, and if Jake is to be believed, it sounds like mine is definitely not.

With the oats gone and nothing left to do but face the music, I grab my purse and head down to the parking garage. My little red roadster is a welcome sight as I make my way over to it, slide inside, and turn on my dance music. There is no traffic to distract me as I make the short drive to work, dancing along with the music in an attempt to lift my spirits and take my mind off what my father wants to meet about. If the business is in trouble, I may have to look for another job. The dread I expect to feel at that thought doesn't come. Instead, I think about how I could use my skillset elsewhere. Maybe I could start over, finally leaving the party girl firmly in the past. My chest balloons with something akin to elation as I think about finally being able to figure out who I really am, deep down inside.

After parking my car and hopping on the elevator, I'm finally at the thirty-fifth floor. When the doors open and I step out, my eyes wander around and take in the sight before me which is nothing but an unoccupied receptionist desk standing in front of a sea of empty cubicles. It's just past 7:00, so it's not surprising to see that no one else is here, but if the business is in trouble, people would be swarming around like angry wasps. Confused, I make my way towards the corner offices, my heavy feet practically dragging behind me. When I see that my dad's is the only one with a light on, I suddenly wonder if maybe it's not the business that's in trouble, but me. Confusion turns to dread as my fist raises to knock on the door jamb, but I pause when my father's light brown eyes meet mine and he waves me in, rendering my announcing myself useless.

"Come in, Biliyana." We're completely alone, but he's speaking in English. It's unsettling, and that rock in my gut sinks further still, anchoring my feet to the floor.

When he sees I'm not moving, he smiles at me, though it doesn't quite reach his eyes. "Please."

"Okay." My voice sounds small, childlike, as I step over to the chair in front of him and take a seat. It seems my ability to fake confidence doesn't work with my dad, though I already knew that. Daddy's girl is also up there along with all of the other descriptors for me. Anytime I was in trouble or anytime I was sad, I would go to my father and he would make it all better. A kiss to the tip of my nose could heal a skinned knee or a broken heart, but I have the feeling it's going to take a lot more than that to fix whatever it is that I broke this time. "What did you want to meet about?"

Tall and built like a bear, my father is an imposing figure, but it's the stoic expression on his normally affable looking face as he gathers his large hands together on his desk that has me feeling intimidated. "You took the owners of Foster Transportation out to a comedy club last night. Is that correct?"

A relieved sigh escapes my previously tight lungs. There is no way I could be in trouble about anything that happened last night. "Yes. We went to see the Chuckleheads. It's an improv group. Everyone had a great time," I explain. The owners didn't participate as much as I thought they would, but they also hadn't had as much to drink as some of the other audience members, so maybe that's why. "Did they want me to get them tickets to another show?" It's not uncommon for clients to want to hit the places I take them to again, and I'm happy to use my connections for them, even if being everyone's nightlife guru has gotten tiresome.

"No, Biliyana. They don't want more tickets," he explains. His tone is dark and his expression even more dour than it was seconds ago as he rakes a hand through his silver hair, giving me a pointed look. "They were highly offended, not only by the content of the show, but by the fact that alcohol was served."

My jaw drops because I can't think of anything in the comedy show that I would deem offensive, though my humor is a little crasser than other people's. And why alcohol? It's not like I forced them to drink, and since I was driving I stuck to my virgin daiquiris. "I don't understand. They seemed to have a good time." Didn't they? Maybe I had a great time and was so caught up in that that the other two people sort of faded from my concern. My interest in my job has waned quite a bit, so that might have affected things as well.

My father gives me a stern look, and I swallow thickly at the sight of it. "Mark Foster is a recovering alcoholic and his wife is a devout Christian. You should have taken them to the symphony or something like that, not a low-brow comedy show," he explains gruffly.

A scoff comes out before I can stop it. "It wasn't low-brow, and I'm sorry, but how was I supposed to know those things about them?" It's not like there was a big flashing sign over their heads announcing that information, and it's not exactly the type of thing you bring up in casual conversation.

My father's expression gets even more severe and I know that no matter what the outcome of this meeting turns out to be, things aren't looking too good for me. "It's your job to know these things, Biliyana," he barks out, clearly exasperated with me. I can almost see his disappointment in me coming off in waves as he shakes his head solemnly. Seeing him like this has me flashing back to all the other times I've felt this way around my parents. While trying to live up to my wild reputation, I got into a fair deal of trouble in high school, and the letdown continued when I chose a "party school" over more sensible options for college. The look my dad had back then is the same one I'm seeing now.

Disappointing my parents isn't unfamiliar, but the feeling is as unwelcome as it always is. Thinking that I'm not meeting their expectations is like a tiny stab in my heart, and I once again wonder just what I'm doing with my life. Clearly an apology is in order, but I'm not sure it will make either of us feel any better. My head hangs low and I shrug my shoulder. "I'm sorry. How can I make it better?" If I have to endure a night at the symphony with mister and missus teetotaler in order to get back into my father's good graces, I'll do it.

"Nothing," he says ominously. Standing up and rounding his large desk, my father takes the seat next to me. "It's a million dollar account, and after a long talk with Mark Foster, I managed to convince him not to pull their business from us." My dad sighs and leans back in the chair, his face is resigned when he finally meets my gaze. "Biliyana. I love you more than I love anything in this world, but you're fired. Effective immediately, you no longer work here and you'll have to relinquish your company apartment."

It takes my mind a few seconds to catch up and process the words that just came out of my father's mouth. "What?" As much as I don't love my job anymore, it does provide me with money and something to fill my time. Oh, yes, and a living space that I am apparently going to have to vacate. "It was one mistake," I sputter.

My father sighs again heavily, shaking his head and patting my knee. "It wasn't just this one mistake, my treasure," he tells me, slipping back into Bulgarian. "For a while now, both your mother and I have noticed your light dimming. You were always so happy, so full of life. Lately, it is like you are a ghost of your former self."

PRACTICE MAKES PERFECT

My throat clogs with emotion and tears prickle at the corners of my eyes as I realize that perhaps I haven't been hiding my feelings as well as I thought I had. My parents have known me my whole life, so it would make sense that they would detect a change in me. Blinking back the moisture that threatens to spill over, I rest my hand on top of his. "How am I supposed to fix that when I have no job and nowhere to live?"

My father raises his eyebrow and gives me a wry look. Fine. Maybe I am acting a slight bit overdramatic, but I can't help it. My savings account is large enough that I can live off of it for a long while, so money isn't really an issue. It's more the idea of having nothing to distract me from ruminating on whether or not there's more to me than meets the eye that scares the crap out of me. Self-reflection is tough and something I'm not looking forward to doing, and it will be unavoidable if all I have in front of me is an abundance of time.

"You can always move home with your mother and me." When he sees my eyes widen in horror, my father chuckles lightly. "Or you can take the time you now have to visit Jake. I know you miss him, and maybe a change of scenery will be good for you." He peers at me thoughtfully for a moment. "You are something more than you pretend to be, Biliyana. Maybe now you can discover just what that is."

Am I more than I pretend? The question pops up and has the same effect it always does. A shuddering breath leaves my lungs and a tear escapes my eye at the thought that perhaps I'm not. My finger reaches up to flick away the moisture, but my father is already there to wipe it with his handkerchief. I sniffle and smile sadly at him. "Thanks." After another deep breath and a look around his large office, I stand and walk towards the door.

My father follows suit and when I turn around, he pulls me into a big bear hug, his thick arms crushing me to his chest. "I love you, Biliyana. Go find your light." He kisses the top of my head and sends me on my way. As I walk into my office for the last time and start gathering up what little personal items I've stowed here, a smile comes across my face and I whip out my phone to text Jake.

Billie: **Hope you're free this weekend. I'm coming for a visit.**

A thumbs up is my only reply and I laugh at my best friend's lack of communication skills. Jake isn't shy, but he definitely likes to keep things succinct. Though I have a feeling that when I tell him I plan on staying for more than just a couple of days, he'll have plenty more to say.

****

The slack jawed look on Jake's face is almost picture worthy, but I doubt he'd be pleased if I reached into my pocket for my phone and snapped a photo to tease him with later. We're at the dining room table, and I've just finished relaying the story of the comedy club incident and subsequent firing to Jake and Maya. JJ is here too, but I'm pretty sure he neither understands nor cares about my problems seeing as how all of his concentration is centered on pushing his mashed potatoes around his plate, no desire to give my troubles a second thought evident.

"I can't believe your dad fired you," Jake proclaims, shaking his head. His expression mirrors what I'm sure mine was just a couple of days ago when I got the news. It's still hard to believe my own dad fired me, but after the talk in his office and another with my mom later that night, I'm trying to see it for the opportunity it is. I've spent so much time performing for others that now I finally get a chance to discover a little more about me and what I might really like to do with my life. Feelings of excitement and horror fill me when I think about what I'll find out about myself, but hopefully the uncertainty will fade in time, letting the thrill remain.

"It seems like a bit of an overreaction to me," Maya adds. Grabbing a napkin, she wipes a bit of smeared gravy off JJ's chin while looking at me with sympathy. "It was one mistake."

My shoulder shrugs as my eyes roam around the dining room. The walls are a welcoming, pale gray-purple with family photos covering any space not occupied by the large bay window opposite me. "It was more than that," I mumble, pushing my food around my plate. It seems JJ isn't the only one using his mashed potatoes as entertainment. "Honestly, I've been phoning it in for a while."

"What?" Jake asks, his expression confused. "But you live for that stuff." Jake knows me a little better than that, though to his credit, I have been playing up the party girl persona a lot more since he moved. Worrying him wasn't something I wanted to do, so I may have implied that I was enjoying work and life a lot more than I actually was.

"Eh," I say, putting my fork down. "I liked planning things and making sure people had a good time for the most part, but the job turned into me being a personal concierge for clients' relatives. 'Get me into the society pages, Billie. Where do all the influencers hang out now?' Ugh, it was all just so meaningless." My eyes finally meet my best friend's. "I like socializing with and meeting new people, but what do I care if so and so's influencer daughter gets a hundred more Instagram followers? It was superficial and gross."

The seat creaks under my best friend's weight as

he leans back in it, his expression one of surprise. "Wow. I didn't realize it was that hard for you." Jake nods and scratches at his jaw, more stubble than he used to have growing on his face. He's really embracing the whole mountain town vibe and from the interested gaze his fiancée is shooting him at the moment, it's working for him. "So what are you going to do now?"

A heavy breath blows out through my lips. "That's the million dollar question," I muse, taking a drink of water. It's to quench my throat that has gone dry from worrying about my next move as much as it is a stall tactic because I really have no clue where to start. "First, I need to find a place to live while I hang out in Starlight Lake. Are there any good rentals in town that you guys know of?"

Jake looks mildly offended. "You can stay with us. We have more than enough room now," he insists. He reaches over and grabs his fiancée's hand, looking over to Maya to get her nod of approval.

"Absolutely." Her words echo his sentiment, but I can tell she isn't quite as enthusiastic about having a long-term guest as my friend is. That is all well and good because I have no desire to disrupt their new family dynamic. Having a front row seat to Jake and Maya's perfect romance is also something I could do without because I can't figure out what the hell to do with my life if I'm spending most of my time being envious of their relationship.

"Thank you," I tell them both. My hands reach across the table, giving both of theirs a firm squeeze. "But I am going to pass. You guys are still settling in and I don't want to get in the way. I can find a place to rent or even stay at the hotel in town for a while. I've got the money, so it's no big deal."

Jake doesn't look too pleased, but a wide smile

comes across Maya's face. Something tells me it's not just because I won't be bunking with them, especially since her eyes are dancing with mischief. "I do know where there is a room that recently became available, and you can even have it for free." Jake looks at her and subtly shakes his head, but Maya ignores him and leans towards me, her eyes bright. "You can have our old room."

My eyes widen. "With Carter?" My mouth opens and closes like a fish as I try to think of what to say to this proposal. On the one hand, it would be nice to not be alone, but I also love to flirt with him, and being so close and spending so much time with him sounds like it's a temptation I don't need. I am supposed to be focusing on myself, though, so maybe it will just be something fun to pass the time while I really dig in to "finding my light" as my dad put it. He'll just be background noise while I figure out what to do with my life. *Yeah, right, background noise you want to climb like a tree.* Dismissing the unhelpful thought, I turn to Maya with a serious expression. "Would he be okay with that? I mean, he just got his privacy back. He probably doesn't want a roommate."

"Psh," Maya scoffs, waving away my concern with her hand. "He hates living alone and would be more than happy to have you stay there. Besides, he loves helping people out and would probably be upset if he found out you were renting a place when he had a room you could stay in."

From what I know of Carter, he does seem to like to help others. What I've gleaned from Jake and Maya is that he basically gave up any kind of life of his own to help his sister out, and this wouldn't be nearly as big of a commitment. "Are you sure? Maybe we should call him," I offer. As soon as the words leave my mouth, I want to pull them right back. The idea of living in the same space as Carter, with the possibility of flirty banter and maybe even a stolen glance at him as he leaves the bathroom in nothing but a towel, his skin wet and glistening is too good to risk on his saying no.

"Not necessary." Maya pulls JJ's plate away from him and starts wiping the mashed potatoes from his tiny fingers. "He's on his yearly camping trip and won't be back until late Sunday. You can sleep here tonight and then we can move you into the apartment tomorrow."

"Well … all right." My agreeing to a plan that I already had my heart set on the minute she mentioned it is easy to do. "But I won't stay there for free." My fingers tap on the wood table as I think of a way to repay them. They're proud people, so I already know they won't accept money, but maybe they would accept a trade of sorts. Another idea forms in my mind and I smile slyly. "I can work in the store. You've been wanting to spend more time on your crocheting, and this will give you a way to do that. Plus, Carter won't have to take as many breaks from his projects to help out, so it's a win for everyone."

Maya looks thoughtful for a moment. "That does sound nice. You really want to work at the store?" She looks skeptical and when my eyes flick over to Jake, his head is bowed and he's shaking it slowly. This is definitely not the worst idea I have ever had, but I know what he's thinking. He doesn't like me interacting with Maya's brother because he thinks I'm just going to use him and lose him, but that's not my plan, nor has it ever been. Still, I can't blame him for thinking that since I've let everyone in my life believe I'm a little flighty. That doesn't make the fact that he's so ready to believe it sting any less though.

My head bobs emphatically. "I'd love to work at

the store. I'll go crazy with nothing to do and it will be my way of saying thank you for all you guys are doing for me." There are a lot of other more fun ways I can think of for how I can thank Maya's brother, but I shut down that line of thinking quickly. No need to make things awkward with him because then I really will need to find somewhere else to stay. "Thank you so much."

"No problem," Maya says. A happy smile decorates her face as she stands and grabs her son. "I'm going to get this little guy ready for bath time. Say night-night to Billie."

JJ smiles shyly and waves at me. "Nigh," he mumbles before burying his face in his mom's shoulder.

"G'night Little J." Maya and JJ walk out of the room and I turn to my best friend. "One of these days I'm going to get that kid to like me." It may take depleting my savings account to buy out an entire toy store to do it, but it would be worth it to see a big smile painted across that adorable little face.

Jake sighs and tilts his head. "He's not the one I'm worried about liking you," he chides, his tone weary. I knew a lecture was coming, I just thought he would wait until his fiancée was out of earshot at least, but I guess I'm not that lucky. "I don't think you living with Carter is a great idea, but I'll go along with it. Just … promise me that you won't toy with him."

The sting from that admonishment is brutal, but I cover it up with my trademark smile. "I won't toy with him," I vow. Rising and grabbing my plate, I walk over into the kitchen to hide the embarrassment at how little my friend thinks of me. Needing to stifle that feeling, I try for a joke. "That is, unless he asks me to."

There is no need to bother looking back at Jake to know what he's doing. Surely he's shaking his head, his expression dire as he wonders how he can best protect his future brother-in-law from me and my man-eating ways. There's no need for it, though the more I think about it, the less my words seem like a joke. Carter is a grown man and can handle himself. And if he decides that he wants me to handle him a little as well? All the better.

Chapter Five

Carter

Stars are abundantly sprinkled across the inky black sky, crickets sound in the distance, and the cool night air brushes across my face, causing a slight shiver to move through my body as I tilt my head back down and peer across the fire. Camping is something I've been doing since I was a boy. My mother was never big on the activity and neither was Maya, so most times it was just Dad and me. We'd fish at the lake for our food before hiking into the mountains, not ever straying too far from our small town, and we'd set up camp by a creek that ran through the vast sea of evergreen trees.

My dad was a big outdoorsman and taught me everything I know. When he wasn't in his shop or with his family, he was out in nature, soaking up the fresh air and sunshine. As we explored the forest, he would tell me stories from his youth, stories about camping with his own father and how much he enjoyed ice fishing as a young boy. The stories would continue as we ate and talked around the fire, me sharing bits of my life with him before he would share more of his past and his hopes for the future.

We camped all year round, only ever canceling our plans when the weather was truly too rough or dangerous. When I was a teen, I asked him why he wanted to come out to the mountains so often. In response, my father would smile gently at me before divulging that a sense of tranquility, of being grounded is what he was seeking. Then he would touch the valknut pendant that was strung around his neck and now belongs to my sister reverently with his fingers and tell me that while our family made him whole, at peace with the world, that coming out into the mountains helped clear away the chaos that could accompany life. He talked about how being one with the natural world gave him the steadiness and strength he required to be everything we needed him to be—a good husband, father, and provider. Being only around thirteen at the time, I didn't fully grasp what he was talking about, but now that I'm thirty-years-old, I have a better understanding of what he meant.

When I come out here and set up camp, everything gets left behind. My worries and obligations just sort of fade into the background, and I feel more at peace with myself. There is no noise from the town, no people out here besides me, but I don't feel lonely like I do when I'm at home in my empty apartment. I'm not a spiritual person, but I feel closer to my dad when I'm out here too. Memories of him are all over these mountains, and as painful as it can be to think of him sometimes with the loss of his influence and support being too great to bear during those moments, it would be more painful to never connect to this place or those memories again.

One night when I was feeling particularly low, I confessed to Maya that I come out here and speak with our father. She didn't tease me about it, but told me she does the same thing, speaking to our mom in the still hours of the late night or early morning in her bed. It felt good to hear that I wasn't alone in still feeling that connection to our parents and needing to keep it going. And I do need it. Now more than ever.

My eyes stare into the flickering orange flames of the small campfire and I shift in my chair. A tree rustles nearby and the sounds of a rabbit or raccoon scurrying away reaches my ears. Ignoring it, I settle in and after clearing my throat, I take one last deep breath and close my eyes. "Hey, Dad," I say to the darkness that surrounds me, "I could use a little advice."

Sounds of the forest are my only reply, not that I expected anything else. After so many years of doing this, I've given up on a replica of my father appearing in the clouds, a la *The Lion King*, ever happening. "I'm not really sure what to do. There are things I want, very badly in fact, but I'm afraid to go after them."

My mouth twitches at the corners as I hear his reply in my mind. "And why should you be afraid? You have Viking blood running through your veins, Carter. There is nothing in this world you cannot conquer."

A small chuckle escapes at the reply I had heard so many times, but it doesn't help make things better this time. My father was so proud of his Norwegian heritage and believed that the strength of those that came before him still flowed through his veins. That might be true for him, but it doesn't feel true for me. I blow a slow breath out of my lungs and keep going. "I'm not like you, Dad. You were so strong. You always knew what to do and what to say. You were so sure of yourself and your decisions." I swallow thickly and whisper into the darkness. "I'm not like you."

My father's wry expression as he runs his hands through his shoulder length blond hair is a picture that comes to mind easily. "You are stronger than you know, Carter," he would tell me. His large hand would clasp my shoulder and he would stare at me intently, his icy blue eyes shining as they reflected the fire. "I am not always sure of my decisions, but I am always sure of one thing." He would touch his fingers to the pendant and smile knowingly at me. "No matter what decision I make, I will always have my family to support me. You have people who love you, too. Lean on them and you will get the help you need."

As I think over the words he would be sure to say,

I huff a breath and open my eyes, staring above the fire and into the dark forest. "I don't have anyone," I say automatically.

As soon as the words spill from my mouth, a feeling of guilt and disappointment in myself settles over me, making my shoulders heavy. I'm sure my father would be disappointed in me as well. Family was everything to him, and while my parents may be gone and I may not have a partner, I do have my sister and my nephew. Even Jake has been surprisingly cool, insisting on repaying me in small ways for all I did to help Maya and JJ when he wasn't around or wanting to hang out and get to know me better. Aunt Sue may not be in town, but she's also only a phone call away whenever I need some advice from a parental figure. Maybe I do need to ask for more help from them. Asking my sister and her fiancé for dating advice is pretty mortifying, but I can deal with that if it means they can help me get it together enough to find a person of my own.

My phone weighs heavy in my pocket. Thinking of a person of my own has my thoughts drifting to Billie again and while the desire to check her Instagram page is there, I can push it aside for now, mostly because I don't even have enough of a signal out here to access it. What I can't brush aside is the feeling that there is something different, something special about her. Instant attraction aside, Billie is also an incredibly dynamic individual. There probably isn't a single person who she interacts with that doesn't immediately fall a little bit in love with her. Even JJ, who shies away from her and who she is convinced doesn't like her, is totally intimidated by the beauty and light that seems to radiate from her every pore. My nephew may look exactly like his dad, but he's a lot like me, shy with unfamiliar adults and unsure of himself at times. At least I can see him becoming more confident as he ages. The same cannot be said for me. Maya is always telling me I need a confidence boost, something to stop me from overthinking things and focusing on my good qualities. Maybe it's time I actually take her words to heart and let her help me out. With a final look around the forest, I smile wistfully.

"Thanks, Dad," I say to the space in front of me. Even though I know he's only here in spirit, I can still feel the ghost of one of his strong bear hugs wrapping around me and letting me know that everything will turn out for the best.

****

The hike back through the forest and to my car was long and sweaty, the cooler temperature from overnight having burned away the moment the sun peaked up over the horizon. High altitude means cooler weather in the winter and summer, but being closer to the sun means it feels as if your skin is being singed by a laser anytime the light hits it. I ditched my flannel not long after I started my hike back and even that wasn't enough to keep me cool. My hands pluck the damp material of my t-shirt away from my body in an attempt to get some air flowing to my skin, but it doesn't help nearly enough. Luckily after a short drive, I'm finally back to the apartment and can hop straight into the shower.

After walking through the door, I kick it closed and unceremoniously drop my hiking pack and toe off my shoes. One bonus of living alone now is that I don't have to worry about tripping hazards for JJ or cleaning up after myself immediately in order to be a good influence on him either. The apartment feels cooler, but it's not enough. An icy glass of water sounds good right now, but I feel so grimy and gross, the sheen of sweat on my skin making me feel sticky that I put it off. Shower first, then it will be time to rehydrate. As I peel my shirt up and over my head, I let it hit the ground with a moist plop and walk over towards the bathroom. My belt clinks as I start to unbuckle it, but movement out of the corner of my eye has me turning and screaming like a small child.

When I notice another person is in the room, my eyes widen at the sight before me. Sitting on the blue sofa is Billie, a computer tablet in her hand and a wide grin on her face. She looks every bit as beautiful as the last time I saw her, and for a moment I wonder if I am hallucinating from the heat and exertion of the hike. "Billie?" I ask incredulously. As my skin cools, I suddenly feel every bit of my half nakedness as I stare dumbly at one of the most stunningly gorgeous women I have ever seen. My hands fumble as I reach down and start to rebuckle my belt, and when my eyes meet hers once more, a slight pout forms on her full, rosy lips.

"Ah, don't stop on my account." Her expression is sly as the words drip from her mouth like honey. "You were just getting to the good part. Though to be fair, on you they're all good parts." She winks at me and I can feel my body flush, only this time it isn't from the heat of my outdoor excursion.

"What… how…?" My tongue feels twice its normal size as I process her words. I'm fumbling and so inarticulate it's embarrassing, but I can't help but smile just the slightest bit at her flirting. That's all it is, but it feels good, nonetheless. Women don't flirt with me, or if they do, it's not obvious enough for me to notice. Billie makes it obvious in such a way that I'm sure to never miss it, a move I appreciate. As she continues to stare at me, I feel my nipples pebble from the cold and the attention.

Moving over to where I tossed my shirt, I snag it off the floor and put it back on as quickly as possible, not caring whether or not it's inside out or about the fact that it is still incredibly damp. My eyes move to Billie's and if I didn't know better, I would say there was a slight bit of disappointment shining from them. "Why are you in my apartment?" On any other occasion, I would be pleasantly surprised to see her here, but I don't like being caught out as I'm undressing, especially not in front of a woman so completely out of my league.

Billie tosses her tablet to the side and it hits the couch cushion with a soft thud. She stands and walks towards me, playing with the end of her long braid as her slender form sways from side to side. She's wearing some kind of bodysuit that hugs her like a second skin. It leaves very little to the imagination, and even though I have imagined quite a bit where Billie is concerned, it seems I never even got close to conjuring up a fraction of the perfection of the real thing. She's all lean muscle and soft curves, and my fingers twitch with the need to reach out and touch her, trace the skin along the delicate line of her neck. When she's in front of me, her head tips up slightly to look me in the eyes. She's close enough that I can smell roses or maybe some other flower wafting off her skin, and I'm tempted to take a deep inhale. The closeness has me wanting to simultaneously take a step back and also one forward. I'm terrified of being this close to her, but at the same time I can't find the strength to pull away.

"I'm your new roommate." Her rich, captivating voice washes over me and I'm so lost in the sound that her words barely register.

"What's that now?" I ask lazily. My gaze is drifting over the olive skin of her face and landing on the milk chocolate orbs that are her eyes. Brown is sometimes thought of as drab, less notable than lighter colored eyes, but Billie's eyes are the furthest thing from dull that you could get. The lightness near the pupil draws you in, but it's the depth of color from the rest of the iris that holds your attention. The color of her eyes is as much a reflection of her personality as anything else. Her friendly and outgoing nature draws you in, but it's the sense of something deeper beneath the surface that keeps you entranced.

A faint smile comes across her lips and she shakes her head at me, lightly rolling her eyes. "No one ever listens to me," she confesses.

While her tone is teasing, I feel like there's a deeper hurt there that I'm curious about. Why would no one listen to this amazing woman? Her hand reaches down and grabs onto mine, pulling me over to Maya's old room. It's a good thing she's steering me along because my mind is spinning, stuck on the softness and warmth of her skin against mine as well as the fact that a little zing of electricity seemed to shoot up my arm the minute she touched me. My mind is so focused on the feeling that I'm liable to walk straight into a wall if she doesn't prevent it. Finally, she stops at the doorway and I peer inside. For the last few weeks, this room has been basically empty of everything except a few hangers in the closet. Now, there is a fully decorated bedroom inside. A large bed with a pink duvet stands in the center of the room with two mismatched white nightstands topped with slender lamps acting as sentinels on either side.

Billie steps into the room, plops herself down on the bed, and smiles up at me. "What do you think? I don't really have a ton of my own furniture, so I bought a bunch from the store and a couple of other places in town. I'm not really sure what style it is, but I'm calling it mountain chic," she explains, leaning back on the bed.

Seeing Billie sprawled out on a large bed has my mind wandering to inappropriate places. Needing a distraction, my eyes move away from the temptation on the soft mattress in front of me to a pink chest that sits at the foot of the bed. More pink catches my eye, and I look to the side to see a matching pink dresser standing against the wall with a white tea tray on top of it. The tray itself is rather unremarkable, but two of the items that sit on top of it have my feet moving closer. Reaching out, I take a hold of one of the small wooden perfume bottles I made a few months ago. It's small, fitting in the palm of my hand. The floral pattern I stenciled on the top looks as good as I remember. I'm no artist, so I was a little worried that I would muck that part up, but as it turns out, I did a great job.

When I face Billie, she's biting her lower lip, her expression a mixture of guilt and embarrassment. "You're PO Box 153?"

She winces slightly and moves from the bed, taking the bottle from me and holding it to her chest. "Yes," she sighs. She clutches the bottle tightly a moment longer before she reverently places the item back on the tray. "I wasn't hiding my identity on purpose. It just seemed easier to do it that way. No pressure to make something perfect for a friend."

I chuckle slightly. "Is that what we are? Friends?" With someone like her, I would love to be so much more than that, but I know that's impossible. The number of friends I have is few, so if she wants to be counted among them, I'm not going to stop her.

"Sure," she says with a shrug of her shoulder. "I mean, I know we don't know each other too well, but I've heard a lot about you from Jake. Between that, my light Instagram stalking, and the custom items I've had you make for me, I think we could consider ourselves as friends. Especially now that we're living together."

"Yeah, about that." I rub the back of my neck,

pulling a face when I feel the dried sweat there. With the shock of my unexpected guest, I momentarily forgot how gross I still am. "How did that come about exactly?"

Billie's shoulders slump and she bites her lip again. "You're not mad, are you? Maya said it would be okay." Her looking uncertain of herself for the first time since I've met her throws me a bit. She sighs and sits back down on the edge of the bed, staring down at her hands before meeting my gaze once more. "I kind of got fired and lost my apartment. Jake and Maya offered their house, but they just moved in and are all 'perfect little family,'" she says, sounding wistful. "I didn't want to disrupt that."

A humorless chuckle escapes as I shake my head. "I get that," I tell her. I almost join her on the edge of the bed before I remember how dirty my clothes are and remain standing. "They invite me over for dinner all the time, but I don't want to crash the happy family party."

"Exactly." A knowing smile spreads on her face before it falters slightly for a moment. "I have a ton of savings and can find something else. Living here with you just sounded like a lot more fun that living on my own, but I really don't want to impose on you, Carter."

Is a gorgeous woman living with me an imposition? No, because she raises the aesthetic appeal of the place tenfold and likes to have fun, but also yes because I feel out of sorts whenever she's around. That doesn't mean I'm going to kick her out though. "No worries," I tell her. My hands get stuffed into my pockets before I do something silly like reach out and touch her in reassurance. The need to provide touch comfort has never been as strong with anyone as it is with her, and it's a little disconcerting. "It will be nice to have a roommate again. After living with JJ for so long, it's felt too quiet lately." It won't be too bad. My work keeps me pretty busy, and I'm sure Billie will have plenty to do. We'll probably barely see each other.

She sighs with relief and smiles brightly at me. "Well, I'm not too loud of a person. And as a thank you for letting me stay, I'm going to help out in the shop. Give Maya more time to work on her crocheting and all that."

My mouth opens and closes for a moment before I can form a reply. "Great," I squeak. My voice sounds about an octave too high, so I clear my throat. "That's great. Well, I better clean up and then we can talk more."

Before she can reply, I turn and beeline over to my room and grab some clean clothes before rushing into the bathroom. After I turn on the faucet, I rest my hands on the counter and stare in the mirror. My expression is shell shocked, a perfect reflection of how I feel. How am I supposed to start dating when the one woman I've ever been instantly attracted to, the one who throws me even more off my game that usual, is sleeping in the next room? With a sigh, I strip off my soiled clothes and step under the spray and try to give myself a little pep talk. I can do this, I just have to focus on trying to find my person and remember that Billie is firmly in the "never going to happen" box. That's easier said than done, especially when I'll also have to try and ignore the new and exciting feelings she stirs within me.

Chapter Six

Billie

Carter's quickly retreating form brings a frown to my face as I slump back onto the mattress of my new bed. He seemed so flustered at the end of our conversation that I get the feeling he might not actually want me here. Or maybe he doesn't want me helping at the shop? My eyes roam around the light wood of the ceiling and I contemplate how to deal with my skittish roommate. He doesn't know much about me beyond my flirting and anything Jake has told him, which probably hasn't been much.

The sound of the shower turning on has my gaze flicking to the wall that's shared with the bathroom. My eyes squint as I try to see beyond the drywall and plaster, wishing I had x-ray vision. My mind's eye starts to conjure up images of Carter soaping himself up and washing away all traces of his time outdoors. While I love seeing him look squeaky clean, his coming into the apartment covered in a bit of dirt and smelling like the forest was something I wouldn't mind seeing more often either.

And when he whipped that shirt off and revealed so much tan skin and muscle? God, I practically melted into a puddle and had to bite down on my knuckles to keep quiet. He's not chiseled like guys that grace the cover of magazines. His arms are bulky and his torso is a slab of hard muscle, and there isn't as much definition as if he spent hours in the gym, but he's fit, and he looks a whole lot more real than some of the Ken dolls I've been with in the past. Then he started to take off his pants, and while I would like to claim that I would have been a good girl and stopped him from shucking those filthy jeans, I suspect that my desire to know the answer to the boxers or briefs question would have won out.

With a shake of my head, I sit up and hop off the bed before my mind can wander down that road any further. I'm turned on enough already as it is and don't need to add 'caught masturbating' to our awkward roommate bingo card.

My feet carry me out into the kitchen to grab a glass of water, and my eyes catch on the grocery list and meal planning calendar that I saw yesterday when I moved in. Maya explained that it was Carter's idea, something to keep them all organized when they were always busy with the shop and taking care of JJ. As I look over the scrawling letters of his list, an idea hits me. He's probably worried that I'll be a terrible roommate, or that I won't know what I'm doing at the store. After everything he's done for his family, Carter doesn't need another project on his plate, and I'm sure he's worried that's what dealing with me will be. A big, annoying, hot mess of a project. Well, I may not be known for being the most practical person in the world, but I can certainly focus and make sure I'm the best damned roommate slash coworker he's ever had.

Opening the refrigerator, I check to see what's inside in hopes that I can scrounge up something to make for dinner. Best cook in the world is not a title that I will ever hold, but I know enough about preparing food to get by, even having the skills to make a few of my mom's favorite Bulgarian dishes. When I open the vegetable crisper and see tomatoes, cucumbers, and some peppers, I decide to make shopska salad. It's a pretty warm day out, and something light and crisp like the native dish will be perfect. Finding some chicken breasts, I decide to throw together a marinade and get that going as well so that I can cook them up for dinner this evening. It will be quick, easy, and best of all, Carter won't have to lift a finger. Tonight, I want to prove that I can be a great roommate and tomorrow I can prove what a competent worker I can be.

Pulling out my phone, I switch on some deep house music from one of my favorite European deejays and dance around the kitchen while I work on my dinner prep. Nightclubs may not really be my scene anymore, but the music is something I won't tire of anytime soon. The fast tempo and solid base line have me twirling from one side of the kitchen to the other, my booty shaking all over the place. Peeking my head into the fridge one more time to see if I can find any lemon juice, I startle when I pop back out and see Carter standing on the other side. "Shit!" The lemon juice container falls to the floor as I clutch my chest and try to catch my breath. "You scared me," I tell him. Watching as he adorably tries to stifle the smile that I know is just begging to spread across his face does nothing for my racing heartbeat.

Carter bends down to grab the lemon juice and pops back up, handing it over to me with a smile. Our fingers brush and I feel the same sparks that shot up my arm earlier making themselves know again. Maybe it's just static electricity, but by the way Carter flexes his fingers as he draws his hand back, I somehow doubt it. He feels it, too, a thought that is both comforting and scary. "Sorry," he says, his low voice calming me. "Didn't mean to startle you." He grabs a glass from the cabinet and fills it with ice water.

As he gulps it down, I watch his Adam's apple bobbing up and down like it's the most fascinating thing in the world. Right now it is, except then I notice he's wearing a fitted white t-shirt and gray sweatpants, and suddenly all I can think about it how good he looks in the casual clothes without a single oversized flannel in sight. The shirt stretches beautifully across his chest and as

Carter turns to refill his glass, I can see that his pants fit just as well, clinging to the nicest ass I have seen in a very long time, possibly ever.

"No worries," I mumble, suddenly in need of cooling off myself. Grabbing my own glass, I drink and we have a bit of a stand-off, neither of us talking, both of us just staring at the other. The silence isn't awkward, it's more … exploratory, like we're sizing each other up. For fun and because flirting is basically my standard operating procedure, I pop my hip out a little and run a finger across my chest. Carter's eyes follow both movements, but then his eyes narrow and his lips purse. Even though I'm sure it's slightly due to annoyance with me, the expression is sexy as hell and I want to see it more often.

"Making dinner?" he asks, nodding his head to the counter that's covered in half chopped ingredients and the marinating chicken. "You don't have to earn your keep, you know. I'm happy to have you stay here."

My feet, of their own volition, but not to my dismay, move two steps closer to him. The scents of cedar and sandalwood hit my nose. He's around wood all day, so it's no surprise that he smells like it, but what is surprising is my reaction to it. The scent rolling off his body is as alluring as it is comforting, and it's making me want to curl up in his lap for a hug followed by a lengthy make-out session pronto. "Happy to have me stay here?" My head tilts and I narrow my eyes a bit to truly gauge his expression. Keeping my hands from running themselves up his chest is a trial, but I prevail. *Barely.* Finding someone around town to help take the edge off my libido before I accost my new roommate might become necessary if the way my body keeps reacting to Carter is any indication. "Just how happy are you, really?"

Carter looks a little dazed as we stare at one another, and when his eyes dart to my mouth, my eyes widen in reaction. Before I can dwell on that action, however, he begins talking and I find myself staring at his mouth in return. Plump lips stare back at me, and I'm suddenly incredibly curious as to what he tastes like. "I can't really put a number on it. I'm just … happy," he confesses. His eyes close briefly before he clears his throat and steps away from me. "What can I do to help with dinner?"

Whatever weird energy was passing between us seconds ago has vanished, and I decide not to push things. That would be bad roommate etiquette and my ego is a little fragile after the whole getting fired debacle, so I'm not sure I could handle the rejection that would certainly come if I made a pass at him right now. "Want to be in charge of chopping? We're making shopska," I explain. Pointing at the cutting board, I gesture for him to take over while I busy myself with grabbing a large bowl to toss the salad in.

Carter's brow furrows, but he does as I ask and starts halving the cherry tomatoes, picking up smoothly from where I left off. "What's shopska?" he asks. His strong hands make quick work of the tomatoes, and for a second I'm stuck staring at the large, capable appendages while noticing how good the gold of his skin would look against mine as he held me. He slides the vegetables from the cutting board into the bowl and picks up a cucumber, breaking the hypnosis I was momentarily under. "Sliced in halves?" he asks, waving the vegetable at me.

I'm sure there is some kind of crass joke I could make as he grips the cucumber, but I let it pass, proud of myself for my newfound maturity. "Quarters." I smile and get a pan ready for the chicken. "And shopska is a Bulgarian salad made with tomatoes, cucumbers, peppers, and sprinkled with cheese. My mom makes it in the summer when it's particularly hot out." Memories of long summer days spent running around the neighborhood and getting into all kinds of trouble while I waited for Jake to come home from whatever music class or space camp his parents had him enrolled in flood into my brain. If only this summer could be as carefree and easy as the ones I had back then. Shaking the fog of the past off me, I realize that shopska isn't the only thing I have to offer. "In the fall and winter I can bust out some of her stew recipes or one for stuffed grape leaves. They taste heavenly."

My gaze meets Carter's and he smiles wryly. "Plan on staying that long, do you?" His tone is teasing, and he actually doesn't seem horrified by the prospect. *Interesting.* The playful expression on his face is one that I want to see more of, and I will definitely be analyzing the reason for its appearance in more detail later on, but for right now, I need to answer his question before he realizes just how deep my crush goes.

Playing things off, my shoulder shrugs as I place the pan in the oven. "Not sure, actually," I tell him. It's not simply a ploy to remain casual. I honestly have no idea how long I'll be sticking around. Is there a timeline for getting your act together or whatever it is I'm supposed to be doing with my free time? Something tells me that even if I have a sudden epiphany about my life's purpose tomorrow, I'm going to want to stick around a while longer. I could try to convince myself that it would be for Jake and JJ, but I know it would have more to do with the man standing next to me. Pursuing Carter would be a fruitless endeavor, but it would be a fun one, and after pretending to have fun for so long, I could use a little of the real thing.

"I've kind of been spending the last two days

ignoring the whole fired with no apartment thing." It's been nice to disregard the swirl of emotions that those events have caused, but I'm going to have to face them sooner or later. By the confrontational look on Carter's face, it looks like sooner just arrived.

"Why did you get fired?" he asks, scooping cucumbers into the bowl and moving onto the peppers. With a heavy sigh, I fill him in on the meeting with my dad, skipping the part where I almost started crying because I'm having a bit of an existential crisis. When I'm done, I gaze over at Carter and see that his expression looks as shocked as his sister's did when I told her. "That seems like an extreme reaction for one mistake."

My teeth dig into the side of my cheek to postpone admitting to the whole truth, but I might as well get it all out in the open now instead of doling it out in small doses. Being forced to think about it over and over again sounds more torturous than just putting everything out in the open. "I think it was less the mistake and more that he's disappointed. Well, not disappointed so much as worried," I confess, my voice small. "He doesn't think I know who I am and he wants me to figure that out."

A hand on my shoulder has my eyes on Carter once more, my mouth twitching with a bit of happiness when I see that he has abandoned his task and come to stand next to me. His touch is light, but it instantly has me feeling much more grounded that I did moments ago. What is it about this guy that has me feeling all kinds of wonderful in ways I never expected? "Do you think that's true?" A slight frown appears on his face, and when his eyes flick over to his hand, he drops it as if keeping it on my shoulder would scar him for life. The loss of his touch is felt immediately, and I try to ignore the sadness that creeps back into my chest at the action.

Air tickles my lips as I huff a breath. "I don't

know. Maybe?" My hip rests on the counter as I consider his question. Who am I? It's something I've been wanting to explore more deeply but haven't for fear of what I would find, or rather that I wouldn't find much of anything. Not finding the answer to his question, I pose another. "If I don't know who I am, then how do I figure it out?"

Carter's gaze moves to the window where you can see the mountains that are now almost completely devoid of snow. "I think every person is different, but I can tell you what I do." His brow furrows again before he continues. "On second thought, how about I show you? The shop closes at 5:00 tomorrow. After everything is locked up tight, we can go for a small hike. Getting out in nature always helps me, and it might work for you, too. What do you say?"

Hiking isn't something I've done much of. Most of my exercise comes in the form of Pilates and dancing around my apartment or whatever club I happen to find myself in, but I'm not opposed to going on a hike, especially if I'm being led by the man next to me. A thought occurs to me, and once again I make sure to not take advantage of his kindness. "Didn't you just get back from camping?" He couldn't possibly want to head back out again after spending a long weekend in the woods.

Carter smiles and shakes his head at me. "Yes, but this will be an easy hike, more like a walk near the lake than anything else. And I enjoy getting outside." He starts chopping vegetables again and peers at me over his shoulder. "If you come, I'll treat you to Frosty Dogs after. They've got the best hot dogs and ice cream in town."

My eyes squint as I look at him. Alone time with Carter followed by dinner and dessert? That sounds suspiciously like a date, but I know better. He's just being helpful and nice because that's the type of guy he is. "Fine." I move to the counter and add some spices and oil to the salad. "But I'm only going for the hot dog," I insist. In reality, the smile on Carter's face when I agree to his plan is the real incentive to do just about anything he asks of me.

****

An annoying beeping sounds from the register, *again,* and I offer yet another apologetic look to the older woman across from me. "I'm so sorry," I tell her profusely. My fingers frantically punch keys on the computer to try and make change for the woman as I try to hide my irritation. Why can't she use a credit card like everyone else? She could have tapped it and been long gone by now, but no, she wanted to pay cash. As I stumble with the sale and continue to uselessly poke and prod the machine in front of me, I grow increasingly impatient with myself. If I am meant to find out who I am, I can start by crossing competent cashier off the list with absolute certainty. When Maya and JJ finally come through the door, I breathe a heavy sigh of relief. "Oh, thank god. Maya, can you help me?"

Jake's fiancée strides over and smiles politely at the older woman who has been staring daggers at me for the last five minutes. "Sure thing. Could you hold JJ for me?" she asks before dumping her son in my arms.

"S-sure," I tell her, holding onto my nephew for the first time ever. JJ is a little shy around strangers, and even though I have tried to come by more often and video chat, he's still been reticent of letting me get too close. Right now, he looks almost peaceful as I hold him against my hip. His expression is still a little dreamy, and I wonder if I haven't been going about this all wrong. Clearly, anytime he's sleepy is the best time to get in some good cuddles with this kid, and I make a note to slip in some more post-nap visits while I'm in town. Addressing the little bundle of cuteness in my arms, I make my voice soft as to not risk disturbing the peace we have between us. "Hey, Little J. Did you sleep well?" He bobs his head sleepily and rests it against my shoulder as he pets my hair. Maya has finished wrapping up with the customer and is staring wide-eyed at the two of us. My head shakes frantically at her. "Don't say anything. You'll jinx it."

Maya stifles a laugh and holds up both her hands at my whispered command. While JJ is docile, I take the opportunity to walk around the room with him, rubbing his back lightly to keep him in a comfortable state. People wouldn't think this about me since I don't get many opportunities to spend time with them, but I absolutely adore children. They are so pure and don't expect you to be an intriguing, interesting, and complex individual, they just want to be cared for and loved. It's not much different with adults really, but growing older adds complications from years of life experiences that are both good and bad. Looking at the little boy leaning on my shoulder, I envy his lack of cynicism in all things, but especially love.

"Silky," JJ says as he pets my hair. I smile at the compliment.

"Thank you," I tell him, reaching a hand up to ruffle his red curls. "The conditioner is imported. Though I doubt I'll be using that much longer. Auntie Billie is on a budget these days." Walking over to the counter, I reach underneath where I stowed my purse and fish around inside until I reach my prize. "Not too tight a budget to not spoil my favorite kiddo, though."

As I present the small stuffed dinosaur to JJ, I revel in the bright smile that plasters itself on his face as he immediately perks up. "Dino," he cries out. His voice is a little too loud considering his proximity to my ear, but I can handle some hearing loss if it means that he's smiling and happy. "Dank oo, Biwee."

My eyes water at hearing him addressing me directly for once, not shying away in the least or hiding his cute face. Finally, I snap out of it, smiling and nodding at him. "You're very welcome." JJ squirms in my arms and I set him down, watching as he runs over to Maya to show off his dinosaur before heading into the office to play.

"He loves dinosaurs." Maya smiles at me. "And you didn't have to do that, but thank you."

"Of course," I tell her, shrugging a shoulder. "I need to use all my tricks to get in good with that one."

Maya shakes her head and gives me look. "No. He just needed time to get to know you. He can be a little shy," she explains. Her gaze moves over my shoulder for a moment. "Not unlike someone else I know."

My eyes follow hers to where Carter has come in carrying a small rocking chair. He disappears momentarily into the storeroom before appearing once more, dusting his hands off against his jeans. His steps falter slightly when he sees me, but he keeps moving, a smile on his face. "How's day one of training going?"

"Great," Maya says a little too brightly. I give her a deadpan look and her expression looks slightly pained. "Well, it's going at any rate. There are just one or two issues we seem to keep getting hung up on." One or two issues is putting a pretty face on it, but since I'm already calling myself six kinds of incompetent, I appreciate her going easy on me.

"Like what?" he asks, moving between Maya and me. Warmth pours off his skin and I find myself leaning closer, wanting to bask in it like a lizard in the sun.

It takes me a few moments to realize he's looking

at me, and I shake my head to clear away my strange thoughts so that I can explain the issue. "Oh. Um, anytime someone pays with cash, I get tripped up on what steps are what and then the computer freezes." Then I panic and start to wonder if maybe I should just smile and try to find a rich husband who wants a trophy wife since there's nothing else going on between my ears, but I keep that little tidbit to myself.

Carter nods thoughtfully. "That's understandable. The system is a little tricky until you get used to it." There he goes being nice again. How am I supposed to not crush on a man who is always trying to put me at ease when my internal freak-out alarm is blaring? "Okay. Let's go through a pretend sale and we'll see what happens." He presses a few keys and gets to the sale screen. Putting his hand on the small of my back, he steers me in front of him, but stays close behind. "Show me what you would do at this point."

Normally when a guy I want this badly is standing as close to me as he is, what I would do is rub myself all over him like a horny cat, but I can't do that here. My eyes flick over to Maya, noting the knowing smile on her face. Ignoring it and her, I punch in the keys for a cash sale and the beeping sound happens again. "Ugh. I'm hopeless," I whine, covering my face with my hands. When I can't get something as simple as a cash sale right, it's hard not to feel like anyone who ever thought of me as nothing more than a pretty face was right. Sometimes I wonder how I even got through school before remembering that charm and personality go a long way with professors when you need leniency on missed assignments, but that won't work here.

Carter grabs my wrists and brings my hands down to the counter. "Not hopeless," he censures lightly His head is next to mine, and when his breath fans against my cheek, I smell cinnamon and clove. Is that his gum or how he naturally smells? Either way, my mouth starts to water as I think about getting a taste. "You're just getting the order a little mixed up. Its sale, cash, complete, enter. Not cash, sale, enter, complete." Completely oblivious to my inappropriate thoughts about running my tongue along his lips, he grabs a post it note and scribbles the order down before sticking it to the monitor. "There. Now you have a reminder until you get the hang of it."

When I peek over at him, he's smiling gently at me and even though he helped me with something so simple, I still want to hug the crap out of him for being incredibly patient with me. "Thank you," I prattle at him. I lick my dry lips and watch as Carter tracks the movement of my tongue.

"Anytime." His voice is a little rough as his gaze never strays from my mouth.

JJ peeling out of the office making dino noises causes us to jump back from one another. "Hey, Little J." Carter calls out to his nephew before scooping him up in his arms. The spell that seems to settle between us at times is once again broken, and I am left to wonder why it keeps happening. "I have a few minutes before I have to go back into the workshop. Want to play?"

"Play a-me, Carda," JJ exclaims. Soon he's clapping his hands on his uncle's cheeks and squeezing them tightly. "Bi-wee got me a dino." JJ takes his new toy and smashes it on top of Carter's head, causing him to break out in a laugh. The low, melodic sound is nice, and one I wouldn't mind hearing more often. Seeing the two of them interact is always so sweet, and it's giving me ideas about a family of my own.

"Well, that was very nice of her," Carter remarks, looking over at me and nodding. "We still on for that hike later?" When I nod eagerly, he smiles and heads into the office with JJ.

Exhaling slowly, I stare at the space that Carter occupied for a long moment. Maya steps up next to me and I jump, having totally forgotten she was there. "So ... you and my brother, huh?" Her open expression does nothing to hide the fact that she is keenly interested in my answer to that question. Luckily, I can be completely honest with her in my response.

A choking sound comes from my throat and I shake my head quickly to dispel any notion of something untoward happening between Carter and me. "No. No, no, no. We're just friends," I assure her. Everything in my body is telling me that it could be so much more than that, but Maya doesn't need to be privy to that information.

Maya hums and nods, but her eyes are bright with mirth. "If you say so." She heads into the office and joins her brother and her son. As I watch the three of them play, I can't help but picture a very similar scene from sometime in the near future. Only this time, it's Carter, me, and a little boy with green eyes and dark brown hair. Reeling from that strange image, I bump into the counter. *Where did that come from?* The question plagues my mind while my heart tugs at the vision. It would be lovely if it were real, but I'm supposed to be working on finding myself. Putting thoughts of that future aside, I turn around and try to get back to work, but the whole time a question keeps running through my mind. Do I have to be alone to find myself, or could someone I already find myself caring a lot about be part of that journey too? As my eyes once again look over at Carter, I find myself hoping it's the latter.

Chapter Seven

Carter

Normally when I go hiking, most of my focus is taken up by the sights and sounds of the surrounding area. Gazing up at the sky or into the crystal clear lake water that reflects the white wisps of clouds is something I do often when I'm out here, but today all my attention is being drawn to the woman hiking next to me. Even though I keep trying to convince myself that the reason I'm concentrating on Billie is to make sure she doesn't trip and fall, I know the real reason. The trail around the lake is one of the easiest around town, and she isn't having trouble with it, but I am. Billie is … *distracting.*

Her hiking outfit is comprised of tiny biker shorts that cling to her strong thighs and an even clingier tank top that shows off an ample amount of cleavage. It still gets chilly in the evenings, so I recommended she bring a jacket, but she shrugged off the suggestion and insisted that it would "mess up her look." Right now I wish she was a little more into function over fashion because I can't stop staring at all the smooth, olive skin on display. As I once again find myself staring at her, my feet stumble over the nearly obstacle free terrain, but luckily I catch myself before I can face plant into the underbrush near the line of evergreen trees.

Billie reaches over and grabs my arms to help me right myself. "Are you okay?" My cheeks flush with embarrassment and I nod, unable to form words for fear of confessing just how cute she looks with her hair in the long twin braids that rest on her shoulders. Billie's mouth quirks up into a teasing smile, one that I know well and is quickly becoming one of my favorite smiles of hers. "You know, for someone who goes hiking and camping all the time, you kind of trip up a lot."

"I'm normally a lot less clumsy." I rub the back of my neck nervously, hoping that she hasn't discovered the real reason behind my lack of coordination. "Maybe I overdid it this weekend."

Billie hums thoughtfully as she gives me a slow once over. As her eyes trail up and down my body, I feel myself tremble despite the heat of the day. "Well, we have been going nonstop for the last twenty minutes. Do you want to take a break?"

"Sure," I reply quickly. Hopefully a short stop will give me a chance to get my bearings so that I can keep from making a total fool of myself in front of her, the odds of which are increasing exponentially with each passing minute spent in her presence.

We come across a fallen tree that looks out across the lake and take a seat on the soft bark. After digging around my backpack, I pass her a water and take a sip of my own, hoping the liquid will douse some of the flames of desire that flicker in my body anytime I look at Billie. Brushing my reaction off as something that is happening because it's been so long since I've had sex with anyone other than myself is something I could easily do, but I know that isn't the case. There is some enigmatic quality in Billie that I'm really drawn to. She is bright and effervescent, but it's more than that. I highly doubt she would go for someone as reserved as I am, but if I can figure out what it is about her exactly that calls to me, then maybe I can get past it and over the crazy crush that I've developed. Once that's behind me, I can go out and find my real person because there is no way it could be her.

Thinking back on what brought her to Starlight Lake in the first place, I turn to Billie and broach the subject. "So, you came here to find out a little more about yourself, right?"

"That was the plan." Billie turns to me, a wry smile on her face. "I'm not exactly excited at the prospect, though."

My brow furrows. "Why not? Isn't that the point of all this?" My hand sweeps across the expansive scene in front of us. "Life is all about finding out who we are and where we fit in the world, our own smaller worlds and the larger one as a whole."

Billie sighs next to me. "I guess." Instead of focusing on the gorgeous view of the trees and lake, she studies her hands intently for a moment before her gaze meets mine. "What if I don't like what I find?"

Her expression is slightly pained, and I can't help myself from scooting closer to her to offer a bit of comfort, even if it's only from my proximity. "Why wouldn't you?" Her shoulders bounce and she looks away from me. As she does, I take a moment to really study the woman next to me. She is incredibly beautiful, and she knows it, but it seems like she doesn't see the other amazing traits she possesses beyond that. Sucking in a deep breath, I drag her eyes back to mine with a finger under her chin. "Would it help if I tell you what I've found already?"

"Maybe," she breathes out. Her breath skates across my hand, and I reluctantly drop my arm. This is about making her realize how amazing she is, not about me getting caught up in how even more amazing it would be to hold her in my arms and feel a lot more than just her breath on my skin.

Swallowing thickly, I stare into her chocolate brown eyes, hoping that she can see the seriousness in my expression and hear it in my voice. "From what I can tell, you are a rare individual." Her brow furrows and I smile at her confusion. "I mean that in a good way. You are incredibly friendly, not because you have to be, but because you are great with people and you truly want to spread some of the cheer you naturally possess to others. You care a lot about those you love and aren't afraid to show it, whether that means having to drag Jake back here so he can admit to wanting to be with Maya or doing whatever it takes to get JJ to feel comfortable with you. And you like helping others." I give her a knowing look. "You knew we wouldn't take money for nothing, so you set up a PO Box to help our business, ordering things when you probably didn't even want them."

Billie's eyes dart to the side, and for a moment it looks like she's hiding something, but when she looks back at me, whatever was there is gone. "How can you think all that about me? You don't even really know me all that well."

"Maybe not," I admit. There is a lot I don't know about her and so much I would like to, but we'll get there. We are roommates after all. It's not nearly as much as I want from her, but if it's all I have, I will take it gladly. "But that doesn't change the fact that what I do know about you is all true."

She exhales slowly and smiles shyly at me. "Thanks." Her voice has a feathery quality to it. If it were any lighter, it would float away on the slight breeze that swirls around us. Her gaze turns thoughtful once again as she looks out over the water. "I do like being friendly and helping people. Meeting so many different people was the best part of my job until it turned into just another item on my to-do list."

As she picks at the bark on the fallen tree, I think over what she just said and come up with an idea to maybe help her figure out what she wants to do. "What parts of your job did you really enjoy?"

Billie looks back at me, her eyes bright. "This

might sound dumb, but I loved getting to help put together the client lunches or put up decorations for office parties." Her smile widens and it's impossible for me not to grin along with her. Her happiness is infectious. "I even planned an anniversary party for my parents last year. Getting to set everything up for them and see the look on their faces when they strolled into the ballroom and saw it for the first time was the best part of that night." She bites the inside of her cheek, her expression nervous. "What if ... what if I planned parties?"

She still looks a little uncertain, but I know she's more than capable of doing that if she wanted to. "I think that sounds like a great idea. Party planning is something I can totally see you doing and being great at."

Billie nods, but the happiness that decorated her face moments ago starts to fade. "I would need to come up with a business plan, and maybe get a loan. And then what if I'm not even good at it?" I can see her starting to go down a rabbit hole of panic, so I wrap my arm around her shoulder and pull her closer. Her eyes widen at the move, but she doesn't look unhappy about it, so instead of moving away, I relish this small opportunity to hold her.

The feel of her body so close to mine feels so right and so good that I'm practically on cloud nine, but I try to keep my focus where it needs to be, and that is on reassuring her. "I can help you with the business stuff if you want," I offer. As I think over the other issue, an idea pops into my head. Squeezing her shoulder, I smile over at her. "And JJ's birthday is coming up in a few weeks. You could plan his party and see how it goes. If you don't like it, you can try something else." Staring into her big brown eyes, I try to convey something that I have to remind myself of often as well. "And you are more than what you do, you know."

Billie's head bobs up and down slowly as she processes everything I've just told her. "Okay," she breathes out. Her expression is cautiously optimistic, and I take that as a win. Her eyes search mine and she leans closer, bumping my chest with her shoulder. "I want to help you too. What can I do for you?"

My face flushes as the influx of dirty thoughts enters my brain, so I stand, shake them off as best I can, and start hiking again. "I'm good. We should probably get going." The dirty thoughts morph into sweeter ones, like the two of us sitting near a campfire talking, or Billie and me smiling down at our newborn baby. I'm not sure where these thoughts are coming from but they definitely aren't possible. Maybe they could be with someone else, but she wouldn't want someone like me.

Billie hops up from the tree and catches up to me easily. "Why are you in such a hurry all of a sudden?" She looks over at me and I blush again, and as she clocks it, she smiles and points to my face. "Whatever you're thinking, that's what I can help with." My foot trips and I stumble again. Unable to catch myself this time, I land on a pile of dead pine needles. My hands are scraped up and I'm sure my jeans are torn, but neither of those things compares to the embarrassment I feel as Billie crouches down next to me, her hand lightly touching my shoulder as I sit back on my heels. "I didn't mean to upset you."

Her voice is tremulous and hearing her feel guilty when I'm the one with the problem is sobering. Dusting off my hands, I finally meet her gaze and try to offer a reassuring smile. "You didn't upset me," I assure her. She has me flustered and questioning my ability to function as a normal human being sometimes, but she's never upset me. Blowing out a harsh breath, I figure I might as well confess part of the problem to her. "I was just thinking about what I want for my own future and how I don't really know how to go about getting it."

Billie nods thoughtfully. "Well, like I said, I would be happy to help you. You're helping me out with the apartment and general figuring out my life stuff. Even coming out hiking has already been a big help, so if I can return the favor, I would like to."

There's only one thing I want right now, and admitting to it is difficult, but the sincerity in her eyes has me confessing the truth. "I'm not sure how you can help me be better at dating," I smile sadly and shrug my shoulders. "It's been a while, a long while, and I was never that great at it to begin with." Looking over at the tree line, I wonder if she can see the awkwardness pouring off of me like the waves that lap at the sandy shore of the lake. It wouldn't be surprising as I can practically feel it settling over me like one of my oversized flannels.

When I finally muster up the courage to look over at Billie, her expression is veiled, but it quickly changes into her playful one again. "Oh, I think you'd be surprised with what I can help with," she teases with a wink. Standing, she reaches down and offers her hand to me. I take it, grateful for both the assistance and her lightening the mood. As I stand, I try to ignore the pleasure that fills me every time we touch, finding it difficult. "How about we talk a little about it over some Crusty Dog."

Smiling at her, I hike my backpack a little higher on my shoulders. "It's Frosty Dog," I correct her. Not sure if this is the best idea, I find myself nodding at her suggestion anyway. "And we can talk a little more about it, but I'm not sure how you'll be able to help me."

Billie smirks and loops her arm through mine as we start hiking again. "Don't you worry, Carter," she brags. "Where there's a will, there's a way, and when it comes to doing something for you, there is most definitely a will."

She beams at me once more before turning her attention to the trail in front of us, but just like before, all of mine is solely on her. How can she possibly help me find the person I am supposed to be with, when I can't help but wishing that person was her?

Chapter Eight

Billie

The rest of our hike and the ride to dinner was spent with Carter shooting me nervous glances out of the corner of his eye and me trying desperately not to make things awkward by admitting that he doesn't need help with dating because I volunteer as tribute. I would be thrilled to spend my days dating a man who said such beautiful things to me as he had during our hike. He called me thoughtful, caring, and said so many other nice things that I almost melted into a puddle at his feet, wanting him to scoop me up and keep me forever. Compliments about anything other than my looks or taste in clothing are few and far between, and to hear them from such an amazingly selfless and warmhearted person made them even more meaningful. If someone like Carter can see those things in me, maybe they're in there after all and not just a figment of my imagination.

The fact that he sees all of those qualities and was brave enough to confess his trouble with dating had me feeling all warm and squishy inside, like one of the overheated granola bars he passed me halfway through our hike. I wanted nothing more than to give him a great big hug when I saw how nervous he was. I refrained from doing so because I nearly giggled like a schoolgirl when he slung his arm over my shoulder at one point, so there was no way to predict just how crazy I might come off if we actually had our bodies pressed up against one another.

Peeking over at him as he peruses the large menu hanging from the ceiling of the fast food restaurant we're currently standing in, I can't imagine anyone not having the same reaction I did. How has no one snapped up such a great guy already? The women in this town must be blind or dumb to not want a catch like Carter Johansen. He might not look much like a Viking as his Scandinavian name implies, but I know that when it comes to his family, he fights as fearlessly as one. To me, that is far better than any combination of blond hair, blue eyes, and big muscles.

Thinking of Carter as a Viking brings up a recurring daydream I have of him plundering my shores for treasure. The dreams happen at night too, and I can't even count the number of times I've woken up hot, sweaty, and needy as hell from one of them where he stalks into my village, drags me back to his ship, and claims me as his all night long. Grateful for the olive skin on my cheeks that will hide the blush there, I shake my head to try and clear the unhelpful thoughts. *Save those for later, Billie.*

"What looks good?" Carter asks as we step up to order. *You*, immediately comes to mind, but I don't think he would appreciate the flirty remark right now when he's feeling vulnerable. He does look good though. His shirt and jeans cling to his frame nicely, but I need to focus on the matter at hand and not on how badly I wouldn't mind stripping the clothes from his body and cleaning the hike off of him in our shower later.

Clearing the huskiness from my throat, I glance at the menu I have been ignoring and order the first thing I see. "I'll have the mustard dog and the chocolate shake, please." The cashier types in the order and looks impatiently at Carter. The kid can't be more than sixteen years old, so I can't blame him for the look of irritation on his face. When I was sixteen I was driving around with friends, not slinging hot dogs. Part of growing up with that privilege is why I try to be nothing but friendly to everyone. You never know someone's story and I want to put nothing but good energy out into the world if I can.

"I'll have the kraut dog and a chocolate shake as well." After splitting the bill, we head to one of the few red vinyl booths that are in the small space and sit across from each other. Carter taps the table nervously before meeting my gaze. "What do you think you want your business plan to look like?"

I wave off his question. "I don't need a lot of help with that. Jake can whip one up with me in no time and I'm not even sure I'm going to want to plan parties anyway," I explain. When I catch the disappointed expression on Carter's face, I'm quick to back pedal. I should have known he would want to help me no matter what. "You can be a sounding board for my ideas though. Jake is *so* not creative, and your pieces are basically works of art, so you can help me out by listening to my ideas for JJ's party."

Carter narrows his eyes momentarily, but nods his agreement. "All right," he says. Another teen drops off our food and he passes me my dog and shake. "As long as I still get to help you out."

"Of course." Taking a sip of my own ice cold drink, I try to figure out the best way to broach the subject of my helping him. Carter seemed pretty uncomfortable when we were talking about the whole dating thing, so I need to tread lightly. "So, about me helping you—"

"You don't have to," he interrupts. Suddenly his hot dog has become the most interesting object in the room and his eyes won't meet mine. "It's pretty ridiculous, anyway. What thirty-year-old guy asks for dating help, right?"

When he does finally look at me, I can see the vulnerability in his gaze and my heart aches for him. He looks so defeated, and I can't have my Viking looking like that. He should only ever look happy and victorious, and I can't help but want to be the one to help him get there. "I don't think it's ridiculous at all," I confess, my voice and gaze steady. "If I'm not ridiculous for needing help 'finding myself,' then you aren't for needing help finding your person." My heart aches a little more at the thought of him actually finding that person and me getting left behind, but I want to see him happy, so I can do this for him. "Now, why don't you tell me the problem and I'll see what I can do to help."

Carter rubs the back of his neck and shifts in the booth. "I don't know what the problem is *exactly*." He looks over at me and sighs. "But nowadays you have to be on an app if you want to meet anyone, and I *hate* the apps. It's all so superficial and it seems like the women on them either don't want this," he says, waving a hand over his face and body. "Or they're disappointed when my job turns out to be just making furniture and not felling trees in the woods while shirtless."

"Ah, I see." I take a bite of my hot dog and let the salty taste take my mind off of just how hard his comments hit home for me too. Carter was honest with me, so I can be honest with him in return. We won't be able to help one another if we don't know everything, the good, the bad, and the ugly, so I might as well start by getting it all out in the open. "Well, I am no stranger to the fantasy not living up to the reality for the people I date, so you're not alone."

Carter looks shocked. He drops his hot dog and shakes his head. "I'm sorry, but I'm having a hard time believing that. There is no way that anyone could be disappointed with the reality of you."

His confession has butterflies taking flight in my stomach, and with the earnest expression on his face, I fully believe he can't fathom someone not liking what they get when it comes to me. Huffing a laugh, I smile at him. "Well, you are certainly good for my ego, but it's true. Most of the time people see a pretty, party girl and they're more than a little bummed when they find out that I would rather stay at home with pizza and a movie, or a glass of wine and a good book than hit another nightclub." Thinking back on all the guys I've been with in the past, I can't believe I ever dated them for more than one night. "I still like to go out, but only if I have an actual friend there with me, someone who cares about who I am as a person and not just where I can take them or how good I look on their arm."

Carter nods and leans back in the booth. "Wow," he breathes out. His forest green eyes meet mine and I feel like I could happily get lost in those woods for hours if he would let me. "I'm sorry. That really sucks."

Nodding my head in agreement, I try to remember that this is about helping Carter, not making myself feel better. "It does, but my point was that it happens to a lot of people, not just you." Tapping my fingers on the counter again, I come up with an idea. "I think I have a way to help you get more dates, but before I share it with you, I want you to know something."

Carter leans forward, and I follow, helpless against getting caught up in the pull of him anytime he draws nearer to me. "What is it?"

While there are a lot of ways I could be playful, coy, or tease him to keep things light, I need him to at least know how great I think he is before I divulge my plan. With a genuine smile, I reach over and grab his hand. His palms are a little rough, probably from all the woodworking, but I love the feel of the tough callouses against my soft skin. It's a physical reminder of just how solid a person he is, and I love it. "You are a kind, caring, generous, selfless, and all around amazing guy, Carter." I can't help but smirk at him. "You are also incredibly attractive and sexy." He starts to protest that last fact, but I stop him with a shake of my head. "The fact that you don't see it makes you all the more sexy, believe me. Ultimately, what I'm trying to say is that you are pretty awesome, and if the women on the apps don't take the time to linger on your photo or look a little deeper at the man in front of them, well, that's their loss, not yours."

Squeezing his hand one last time, I release it and lean back in the booth. Confessing all of those things and not immediately planting a kiss on him to convince him it's true afterward is difficult enough without the skin to skin contact. Carter looks slightly shell-shocked, but the corners of his mouth lift into a small smile. "Thank you for saying that."

"You're welcome, but you might want to save the thanks for later because it's time for some harsh truths," I wince. The possibility of hurting his feelings is very real and definitely something I don't want to happen, but I want to be completely honest with him. "Are you ready for that?"

Carter rubs his hands together and nods curtly. "Hit me with it."

Nodding, I gaze at him, my expression serious. "All right, here it comes. Whether we like it or not, the app world is the one you're going to have to live in. Unless of course you feel comfortable walking up to and hitting on a woman at a bar or something?" At Carter's horrified look that confirms my suspicions that he is not into that idea, I move on. "So, that means dealing with the fact that people are visual creatures and are going to judge you based on your appearance. I'm not saying it's right, but it is what it is." Reaching into my purse, I grab my phone and open the social media page for Hodgepodge and navigate to one of the pictures that includes an almost full body shot of Carter. "Take a look at yourself and tell me what you see."

Carter studies the shot for a moment before shrugging his shoulders. "I don't know. Maybe I could do something better with my hair?" He sits back and crosses his arms over his chest. "I'm not joining a gym or going on a diet. I hate fitness centers and like eating what I want."

A choking sound gets stuck in my throat. "I would never suggest that and would be pissed if you tried. I like your body the way it is." When I see Carter's eyes widen at that confession, I plow forward, determined not to make any more embarrassing confessions. "What I was going to suggest was that we punch up your wardrobe a little, or at least get you clothes that fit your frame and show off your body a little better. I mean, your flannel shirts are like two sizes too large."

When Carter's face falls, I get the feeling I've stepped in something I shouldn't have, and as he starts playing with the tattered hem of the flannel that has been tied around his waist all evening, I know I have. When his eyes meet mine, they're filled with sadness and my stomach drops as if the hot dog I ate weighed fifty pounds. "They were my dad's," he says hoarsely. He clears his throat and looks around the mostly empty restaurant before speaking again. "I know they don't fit, but I feel a little more connected to him when I wear them. Flannel was his thing and I know it's dumb—"

"It's not dumb." Grabbing his hand again, I give it a reassuring squeeze and flash a knowing smile. "I get it. It's not quite the same, but the perfume bottles I had you make were something my grandma had in her house in Bulgaria. They got lost a long time ago, so that's why I had you make a set for me and my mom, to help us remember and stay connected to her."

Carter squeezes my hand and we sit for a moment, hands clasped as the weighted blanket of our shared experiences settles over us. "Maybe we can do something like that for you."

An eyebrow quirks in question. "I'm not sure I need a perfume bottle," he smirks.

Shaking my head, I mock glare at him. "Such a smart ass," I sass. I love getting to see this more playful side to him, especially as he seems happier after the tough confession about his dad's flannels. "I meant the clothes. What if we went and got you some plaid flannels of your own that actually fit? You'll still be honoring and remembering your dad while making it your own. Wearing something that you can feel comfortable and confident in can do wonders for your self-esteem. Trust me." I wiggle in my seat and Carter tracks the movement, licking his lips as he does.

His eyes meet mine, and if I didn't know better, I would say they were filled with a little bit of heat. "I do trust you," he admits. His gaze moves away from me, but I can see the smile on his face.

As much as I would love to convince myself that he was attracted to me, I'm too busy reveling at his confession that he trusts me. Carter's trust means a lot to me, I just hope that I don't ever give him a reason to doubt it. Thinking about how flaky everyone thinks I am has me wondering if that's possible. "Great." My voice is tight with emotion and it feels like there's a weight on my chest, but I move past it. "Then let's finish dinner and then we can go through your closet."

Carter's eyes shoot to mine. "What's that?"

My cheeks drift upward as my lips pull into a mischievous smile. "You really didn't think you were going to get through this whole thing without me looking at your current wardrobe and taking you on a shopping spree, did you? Have you never seen a movie makeover montage?"

Carter huffs a breath and shakes his head. "I've seen one, just never thought I would be a willing participant in my own." He wipes a hand down his face, but his expression is more amused than resigned, bolstering my resolve to help him.

Twenty minutes later, we've returned to the apartment and are walking into Carter's room. I've seen bits and pieces of it from the doorway, but I have never been inside until now. "Wow." The exclamation comes as I take a look around the room, my hand running along some wood paneling that has to have been done by the man himself. Instead of the old style where it looks like clapboard pasted onto drywall, the different sized panels are laid out more like bricks, creating a beautiful tapestry of different grain patterns. My hand falls as I take in the rest of the room. It's pretty sparse, and aside from the large bed, dresser, and nightstand, there's not much else in the room. "Where's all your furniture? I figured your room would be wall to wall wood."

He gestures to the wall I was just admiring. "Well, it kind of is, but other than that I don't have a lot of time to make pieces for myself."

My jaw drops as I walk over to his closet. "You literally made a bed frame that doubles as a fort for JJ," I remind him. "You could have been a little less extra with that and done something nice for yourself."

Carter's hands get stuffed into his pockets and his shoulders bounce. "I would rather do nice things for other people."

Sighing, I smile indulgently at him. Of course he would have an inability to be selfish. "Well, if you won't do something nice for yourself, it's a good thing I'm here to do nice things to you." My eyes widen as I realize words just popped out of my mouth. "For you. Do nice things *for* you," I gulp. Burying my head in the closet is a great way to both hide my beet red face and to avoid looking at Carter after my little Freudian slip. As I rifle through his clothes, I see a lot of the same thing—jeans, oversized flannels, and the occasional faded button down. Popping my head back out, I gape at my roommate. "This is pretty dire, Carter. I don't see a single pair of slacks in here."

He plops down on his bed, looking completely unbothered by my declaration. "I don't really have much occasion to dress up," he admits.

I hum a reply as I move over to his dresser. I don't want to think about Carter being lonely, mostly because it reminds me of my own desire for companionship. Nor do I want to think about him having more occasions to dress up, like going on dates with women who aren't me, but I can't be selfish, at least not with someone like him. He deserves someone as great as he is, not someone who barely has any direction for her life. As I search through his drawers, coming across a lot of t-shirts, sweatpants, and the occasional long sleeved Henley, something niggles at my mind until I finally realize what I've been looking for and haven't found. Spinning around, I look at Carter's expectant face. "Where are your boxers?"

Carter shakes his head. "I don't have any," he replies. He offers up no other information, so I'm forced to drag the conversation along on my own.

"Okay. Well, then where are your briefs?" He shakes his head again. "Boxer briefs?" Another head shake. "Panties?" I hedge. Not for nothing, but I definitely don't hate the image of Carter in a pair of my lacy black underwear. He could definitely pull off the look.

Carter coughs and gives me a pointed look. "I don't really own any underwear."

"Oh," I reply. Then his words hit me with the force of a Mack truck and I nearly swallow my tongue. "*Oh*." Carter goes commando, so the other day when he was doing his little striptease, if I hadn't spoken up I would have gotten a lot more than a peek at some underpants. My mind floods with all kinds of images of what I might have seen and how differently that afternoon could have played out had I seen it, and suddenly I need to be anywhere other than in this room with him. The air is stifling, my skin feels hot, and tight, and there is a steady ache between my legs that needs to go away before I straddle the man in front of me and ask him for a helping hand. "I can work with that. I mean, we can work with the whole no undies thing. Your wardrobe definitely needs updating, so we'll go shopping this weekend and get a capsule wardrobe for you. Don't worry about not knowing what that means, I can explain that later." I cringe at the speed of my words and overall awkwardness as I back toward the doorway. "I'm going to go for a walk. Just for a bit."

Carter coughs again, shifting on the bed. When I see the move, I start thinking about how broken in the denim of his pants is and that it probably feels very soft against his bare skin. This is not helpful thinking. "Sounds good," he says, oblivious to my inner turmoil. "Be safe."

My head moves up and down like an out of control bobble figure as I back out of the door. "Yup, totally. I'll see you later." As soon as I'm free, I bolt out of the apartment and head down the stairs. My feet hit the sidewalk hard as I run from all the feelings that my very interesting discovery from minutes ago has stirred up.

The night air does little to cool me as I make the

short walk over to the town square. Spying the fountain that is fabled to have brought magic into the lives of some of the townspeople as well as Jake and Maya, I take a seat at the edge, hoping the mist coming off the running water will help squash my desire. When sitting there doesn't help, I remember that I promised to call my parents. Speaking with them is a sure fire way to get my hormones in check, so I pull out my phone and dial up my dad. I shot off a text when I arrived in town to let them know I was safe, but other than that, he and my mom have left me to my own devices, much like when I was younger.

On the third ring, he finally answers, his loud voice booming Bulgarian greetings through the speaker. "Biliyana! It is good to hear from you, my treasure." The nickname he has called me since birth brings a smile to my face and helps to calm my stormy emotions. "You are on speaker and your mother is here as well. Now, how has your time with Jake been?"

"Good," I answer honestly. What little time I have spent with my best friend has been great, though to be honest I have preferred the time I've been spending with my new roommate. "We haven't had a lot of time to hang out since I just got here and him being so busy with work and JJ, but I'm keeping myself busy in other ways." After filling my parents in on my time at the store today and my hiking adventure with Carter, I explain how I am thinking about moving into party planning starting with my nephew's birthday. When no reply comes across, I pull back and check to see if my phone is still on. "Mom, Dad? Are you there?"

A heavy sigh comes through and I frown at it before I hear the softer tones of my mother's voice. "If that is something you want to do, then your father and I will support you in that, of course, but you sounded so excited when you talked about the store you are working at now or your new friend." I don't miss her emphasis on the word *friend* and make a mental note to not mention Carter anymore so she doesn't get any wild ideas that I haven't already had and dismissed a million times myself. "When you speak about planning parties, it doesn't sound like the idea lights you up," she tells me.

My eyes roll a bit at that because what job lights anyone up? My mind also conjures up images of Jake smiling as he shakes hands with a small business owner, Maya getting all giddy when she finishes one of her crocheted animal buddies for a small child, or Carter's look of pride when he runs his hands over one of his wood pieces. They all seem to have found the thing that lights them up, and I want that for myself. Sure, the idea of planning parties for the rest of my life doesn't sound amazing, but I won't know until I take that first step. Besides, not everyone can love what they do for a living.

Shrugging a shoulder, I focus my attention back on my call. "It might not light me up yet, but we'll just have to see how I feel after the party."

"This is true, I suppose," my mother tells me.

We move on from the topic of my not-so-put-together life over to their very established ones that include the latest win my father had in a seniors' boxing tournament and gossip about my mother's friends. We pointedly avoid talking about my dad's company, and that's fine with me. That part of my dad's life is important to him, so I hope we can speak about it eventually, and there are honestly no hard feelings on my part. It speaks to just how much I had started to detach myself from the job, and I wonder why it took me getting fired for me to finally do something about it.

After we say our goodbyes and promise to talk soon, I hang up and turn to look at the fountain behind me, the light from nearby businesses playing on the water. Wistfully, I gaze at the statue of the two doves in flight, wondering if I will ever be at peace like that with someone next to me as I make my way through life. Jake told me about how he came to Starlight Lake on a whim and wished for something incredible. He got Maya and JJ in return, and while I would love to believe something similar could happen to me, maybe even with a certain woodworker I know, I'm just not sure that's the case. Still, as I pull a dime from my pocket, close my hand around it and shut my eyes, I hope that maybe there's enough magic left here for me.

Chapter Nine

Carter

After the night Billie went through my wardrobe and I subsequently confessed to going sans underwear all the time, we've spent the last few days avoiding the topic of our upcoming shopping trip. That ended last night when Billie announced that we would be going to the outlet center a few towns over to "shop 'til we drop," and now I'm sitting in the passenger seat of her small sports car, wondering what I've gotten myself into. Agreeing to Billie's plan was easy enough, especially after she complimented me and told me I'm sexy. While I'm not sure I totally believe her about that last bit, I'm flattered that she noticed that I like to do things for other people.

Maybe acts of service and gifts is my love language, but it's also something I've always enjoyed doing. Just as Billie enjoys meeting new people and generally being social, I love seeing people's faces light up with glee when they receive one of my furniture pieces or eat one of the meals I've made. Glancing over at the woman next to me, I can't help but want to do so many acts of service for her too.

Beyond helping with her business ideas or letting her stay in the apartment, I want to shower her with compliments about what an amazing person she is and how much happier I've been in the week she's moved in with me. The loneliness is gone, but it's more than that. It's having her at the store and getting to know her bit by bit every time we interact. There are also other acts of service I wouldn't mind performing, like doing whatever I can to make her moan and scream with pleasure until she begs me to stop. But it's been so long that I probably wouldn't even know what I was doing if she ever deigned to let me near her. With a heavy sigh, I turn and look out the window, noticing the large sign for the outlet mall just up ahead.

"Come on, Carter," she chastises me. She's completely misunderstanding the reason for my mood, although shopping isn't exactly the type of activity I get jazzed about. Her hand reaches over and squeezes my knee, a move that definitely doesn't help the arousal I was feeling moments ago. "It won't be that bad. I'll go easy on you, and if you promise to keep the complaining to a minimum, I'll even buy you a pretzel as a reward."

I huff a laugh. My mind was thinking of other rewards, but despite her declaration that she thinks I'm sexy, I somehow doubt she would be down for offering any of those instead. "Throw in some cheese sauce and you've got yourself a deal." I smile over at her, happy when I get one of hers in response.

Ten minutes later, Billie is pulling me along while I drag my feet over to the first store. "I know that you've got a budget, but just remember that you might spend a little more now for clothes that will last much longer than if we went for cheaper options," she explains.

I nod as we head into what looks like a high-end camping store. "What is this place?"

Billie gives me a withering look. "You've never heard of Outside In? It's basically where fashion and the outdoors meet up, have sex, and then spew their gorgeous clothing babies all over the place."

"There's an interesting visual," I quip as we walk around. A salesperson approaches Billie and the two chat for a bit while I get caught up in looking at a pair of silk boxers with pictures of moose all over them. "This is why I don't wear underpants." My feet on the glazed cement floor, my body uncomfortable in the one pair I do actually own and had to wear today since I'll be trying on clothes. Shaking my head, I move over to another section and see a wool beanie that looks somewhat normal. Picking it up, my fingers run across the scratchy material, but I drop it like a hot potato when Billie suddenly appears next to me with an armful of clothes. My mouth gapes at the pile that nearly obstructs her face from view. "How did you grab all of that already?"

Billie smiles and nods over to the salesperson she was talking to moments ago. "I told Craig your sizes and the look we're going for, and he helped me pull a few things." She waves at Craig who happily waves back like he's her new best friend before she starts shoving me toward the dressing rooms. Once I'm inside, she hangs up her finds before grabbing a pair of jeans and a blue and green plaid flannel. "Here, try these on and see how they fit. Then come show me, and I'll tell you how they really fit." With a bright grin, she shuts the door and waits outside.

With as little grumbling as possible, I do as she asks. Once I'm dressed, I give myself a cursory glance in the mirror and find that I actually like what I'm seeing. The colors of the shirt almost make my eyes look greener than usual, and it fits snuggly enough that it shows off the bulk of my arms and chest without being so tight that it's uncomfortable. The jeans are a great fit too. Normally I have to go a size up on pants since I have a bit of a bubble butt, but Billie managed to find some that look good and fit nicely too. "Huh," I say as I twist and turn in the mirror.

"Come one. Let me see," Billie whines from the other side of the door.

With a shrug, I open the door and spread my arms wide. "Well, what do you think?" Billie scrutinizes my look and hums lightly as she walks around me, tugging on the shirt a little here and there. When her hands reach up and start smoothing over my shoulders and chest, I nearly choke on the saliva in my mouth. "What are you doing?"

Billie gives me an indulgent look as she moves her hands up to my neck and reaches into the collar. "Seeing how it fits, silly." I can't remember the last time someone called me silly, and I kind of like it. When I look down and see Billie's sly smile, my stomach drops with anticipation of what she'll do next. "Do you want me to stop?" My head moves from side to side and her smile widens and she runs her hand lower to my waist. Two of her fingers dip just inside and run along my stomach before disappearing around the back. "Do they feel too tight?" I know she is asking me a legitimate question, but I can't help but wonder if she knows that the effect of her touch has a certain part of these jeans feeling a lot snugger than it did a minute ago.

"No." My voice is husky, so I clear my throat to try and sound a lot less turned on than I actually am. "No, they fit well."

"Good," she smiles. Stepping away and fortunately keeping her eyes level with mine, she nods, clearly pleased with her work. "Okay, next outfit."

The next forty minutes goes by much the same as the last ten minutes, and by the time we have established a capsule wardrobe, something Billie explained was a set of basic clothes I can mix and match as well as add other items to, I'm so turned on that I'm afraid I'm going to make a mess in the jeans that I don't yet own. Luckily, by the time I've changed back into my own clothes and made the purchase, I've calmed myself down enough to walk around the rest of the shopping center without the addition of an inconvenient and inappropriate for public consumption erection.

"Should we hit the next store?" Billie asks. She

must read the reluctance on my face and starts steering us toward the food court instead. "I can see that you're already a little tired of all the wardrobe changes, so let's get some fuel for the rest of the afternoon."

I don't have the courage to tell her it's not the outfit changes but her hands all over me that is making shopping nearly impossible, so I nod and we head inside. Billie buys me a pretzel with cheese sauce, telling me I earned it with such a beautiful smile that I decide I can suck it up for the rest of the afternoon and keep shopping if I can earn another of her bright looks. She grabs some pretzel bites for herself and we head back outside to enjoy the mild weather while we eat.

We sit in comfortable silence for a moment, but my phone buzzing with a reminder to finish JJ's birthday present, a wooden dinosaur puzzle, has me initiating conversation. "Maya tells me she okayed you planning Little J's party. Do you want to go over any ideas you have?"

Billie holds up a finger while she finishes chewing before she wipes her butter glistened lips with a napkin. Wishing I were that napkin, I almost miss what she says next. "Sure." She pulls a small planner from her purse and flips it open to a page titled, Little J's Big Three. Smiling at the title, I take a closer look and see a lot of carefully arranged plans and times. Her planner looks a lot like the meal plan I have on the refrigerator, and I smile at the thought that we have something as simple as planning quirks in common.

"I know JJ loves dinosaurs, so I called Kerry at the local bakery and have commissioned a stegosaurus cake, and I went to the party supply store and ordered a slew of dino themed decorations and a T-rex piñata. I talked to Maya, and in addition to Jake's parents, your Aunt Sue, and the two of us, she wanted to invite a couple of JJ's friends from his play group and their parents. Since the littles will need some fun activities, I'm going to put together a few sensory games like digging for dino eggs in the sand box and then they can make a fossil of their own handprint out of salt dough." When she's finished, she bites the end of her thumbnail and looks over at me with an uncertain expression on her face. "Does that sound okay?"

Completely blown away, but not at all surprised by her creativity, I search for the right words to convey just how impressed with her I really am. "That's really amazing, Billie," I spill, barely able to contain my excitement for her. A wide grin takes over my face as pride swells in my chest. "I can't believe you came up with all that so quickly, and that you not only ordered a cake but already know the bakery owner by name. It took me years to remember to call her Kerry and not Karen."

Billie shrugs at my compliments, but the faint blush on her cheeks tells me she's accepted them as truth. "Well, it was nice to go around to the different stores and talk to the owners. The business district seems like its own little family." I nod and watch as a cautious smile paints Billie's face as she looks over at me. "You really think my ideas sound good?" She taps her planner and leans closer, her rose scent wafting over me. Suddenly I want to plant a whole garden full of the flower as soon as possible. "I really just want Little J to have a good time. I know Jake and I aren't blood related, but I really think of him as my nephew and want him to have a great birthday."

I nod my understanding and smile at her. "JJ will have a great time because he will be surrounded by people who love and care about him, which clearly you do, blood relative or not."

"Thanks," she replies, her smile shy. Shyness isn't

normally something you see much of coming from Billie, but it's a good look on her. Her eyes are soft and her face is more open. She is far less intimidating because there is no trace of the flirtatious woman who constantly throws me off kilter there, though I like that part of her too. As it turns out, I'm enjoying just about every part of her and wonder how any other woman I meet will possibly compare. Billie slapping her hands on the table breaks me from my reverie and I look over to see her shy smile has been replaced by an impish grin. "You ready for more shopping?"

Stifling a groan, I gather up our trash and dispose of it. Looking over my shoulder at her, I try for my best hangdog expression. "Do we have to? I already have my capsule wardrobe." I can't believe words like that just came from my mouth, but here we are.

Billie rolls her eyes, and with a shake of her head, she starts dragging me to another store. "Those are just the basics," she explains. As much as I'm not wanting to try on a bunch of clothes, I am really enjoying spending the day together and will happily endure it if it means more time in her company. "Now we need to put together a few date night outfits. Jeans and flannels are good for every day, but you need to dress up a little more when you're out on the town."

"I guess." My mood sours slightly at the thought of going out on the town with anyone other than her. "I would rather someone like me for who I am, not what I'm wearing."

Billie stops walking and turns to face me, her expression determined. "We talked about this, Carter. You're still you," she tells me, patting my chest lightly. There is the temptation to place my hands over hers to keep them there for a while, but I resist it. "This is just window dressing. It gets people into the store and your personality is what gets them to hang around and make a purchase."

I chuckle at her analogy and nod. "Okay then. Let's go get some more window dressing." Billie smiles and we spend another few hours getting me all set up with clothes for every dating situation I could possibly find myself in from fancy restaurant to picnic in the woods, but there was one situation Billie couldn't prepare me for. The one where my crush slowly evolves into something more, knowing that more likely than not, those feelings will remain unrequited.

Chapter Ten

Billie

The party I put together for Little J is in full swing, and it looks like everyone is having a great time, but the only person I care about being happy right now is the boy with the red curls who is currently smashing open eggs to try and find the small dinosaur toys I spent last night stuffing inside. Carter was there, too, of course, spending time he should be working on his dating app profile helping me with my project instead. When I asked him about why he hadn't put it together yet, he shrugged and brushed my comment aside, telling me he would work on it after the party was over. I don't want to come off as pushy, but I *really* need him to start going out on dates soon because him spending all his free time with me is giving me ideas. Ideas that involve a lot more of what happened last week.

The shopping and spending time together was wonderful, and we got to learn even more small tidbits of information about each other. In addition to both being the children of immigrants, we also enjoy quiet nights at home and prefer summer over winter. Over the course of the afternoon, Carter also learned that I hate sunglasses that cover half of my face and need at least two snack stops when out on a shopping spree. To remedy that last need, Carter bought us both an ice cream and we sat on a wooden bench to rest and talk while we ate our cones. We talked about the projects he was working on for the shop and I talked about more of my party plans for JJ, but we also talked about how he reads thriller novels even though he scares easily, and that he thinks deep dish pizza is more like a lasagna, but he still enjoys it.

I talked about my time in college and how it was

basically a blur of parties, and confessed that even though I acted that way a lot in the past, what I actually love to do is eat in front of the television while I watch reality dating shows. After hearing that, Carter has spent every night since then showing me how to make dinner before we watch the latest season of *Love Boat UK,* a dating show where singles literally live on a boat for a month while they look for love but really just end up hooking up with one another. Carter shook his head in dismay as we watched, bemoaning the fact that this is what dating had come to, but I saw him laughing every now and then, especially when the more dramatic contestants would start fighting with one another. I think he secretly likes it just as much as I do.

In addition to the shopping and getting-to-know-you sessions, I got to spend a good amount of our day with my hands all over him. It was a bit torturous, trying to keep things PG as I smoothed my hands over parts of his body to check the fit of his clothes. The first time my fingers grazed the bare skin of his stomach and felt the dusting of hair that comprised his happy trail, a wave of pleasure washed through me. From then on, I had to be diligent about being more careful where I touched him lest I soak my panties or make a fool of myself by pushing him back into the dressing room and trying to have my way with him. Carter is so sexy in a way that he doesn't realize is sexy. He works hard, is so giving, and he listens so attentively any time I talk. After so many years of being seen as just a pretty face, it's nice to be with a guy who actually pays attention to my thoughts and feelings, though he is so much more than that. He is so many amazing qualities wrapped up into one perfect man. That kind of perfection is intimidating as hell, but damn if I'm not drawn to it as well.

Currently, my eyes are drawn to Carter as he

helps Jake sling a piñata over a large tree branch in the backyard. He looks really good in his new clothes. His flannel fits a lot more snugly, giving a better hint at the body underneath, and his pants show off his amazing ass really well too. The best part is that his flannels aren't quite as long now, so when he lifts his arms over his head to raise the paper mâché dinosaur higher, I get a peek of his hard stomach and the treasure trail I had my hands on just a week earlier. Grabbing a paper plate off the table, I fan myself a little to try and cool down from the barrage of heated thoughts that batter my brain. *Children's party, Billie. Keep it clean.*

"You okay there?" Maya asks. When I turn to her, she has a knowing smile plastered on her beautiful face.

While I'm sure that the teensy, okay *huge* crush I've developed on her brother is obvious, I don't need to give her confirmation of it. She would definitely tell Jake and he's already warned me not to mess with Carter. The last thing I want or need is a lecture from my best friend about how I'll just use and abuse his brother-in-law only to disappear back to Denver when I'm done. I don't think that's true, but even the possibility that I could hurt my new friend makes me leery of pursuing anything more or even mentioning my wanting to. "It's just a warm day," I lie. Placing the paper plate back on the table, I turn to Maya and smile. "Are you happy with the party?"

Her head bobs in approval, her blonde hair waving as she does, though she shoots me a look letting me know she's not happy with the subject change. "The party is amazing," she tells me, her wan look melting away into a smile. Nodding down at her son who is busy kicking up sand with his friends, she reaches over and pulls me into a hug. "JJ is having an amazing time, but more than that, it means a lot to me to have other people showing up and caring about him." When she pulls back,

I see her eyes are a little misty, but she blinks it away. "It was just the three of us for so long, but now we have so much more. Thank you."

Getting a little choked up myself, I smile to cover it up. "It's no big deal. Just a party."

"It's a lot more than that," she breathes out. Her eyes are on her fiancé and my best friend, and I know she's thanking me for dragging Jake back to Starlight Lake and back to his family.

"He would have come on his own eventually," I confess. With as much love as Jake had for Maya, I'm sure he would have been back to her within a month of me having brought him.

Maya nods. "I know, but I'm glad I didn't have to wait any longer than I already did."

Her smile grows as Jake walks up to her and pulls her into his side, kissing her temple as he does. "Were you two talking about me?"

"That's incredibly self-absorbed, but, yes, yes we were," I inform him. Jake isn't that full of himself, and it is a good bet that if Maya and I are talking, it would be about the one thing we have in common. My eyes catch Carter crouching down and helping JJ break one of his dino eggs. Maybe we have a few other things in common now too.

Jake looks over at me. "This is a great party, Billie." He pulls me into his other side and gives me a hard squeeze. "I'm really proud of you."

"Thanks." His praise means a lot, especially since he was always the more hard-working and responsible of the two of us. "Maybe I'll do this for a living." The idea doesn't immediately thrill me like I had hoped it would and my eyes flick over to Carter to see him studying me. Not wanting the scrutiny at the moment, I turn back to my friend.

Jake's eyes light up and he nods happily at my proclamation. "I think that sounds like a great plan." The mention of plans coming from him is no surprise, but I'm not fully on board with the party planning train yet to be as excited as he is.

When I turn back to Maya, she's glancing over at her Aunt Sue with a smile. I met the woman earlier and she is just the right amount of sassy while still being funny. "You know, Sue said she would watch JJ so that we could have a night out. Why don't the four of us go out on the town?"

Shock paints my face as I look over at the happy couple. "You want to give up the opportunity of a date night to hang out with me and your brother?" My eyes narrow in suspicion. I smell a set up.

Maya waves off my statement. "I see Jake every day now." When her fiancé gives her a slightly affronted look, she smiles sweetly at him. "And I love every minute of it. But now that we don't live together anymore and I've cut back on my hours at the store, I haven't gotten to spend as much time with Carter."

Her expression looks genuinely distressed at this and I feel slightly guilty for having questioned her motives. "Okay, but only if you let the two of us babysit Little J next weekend so that you guys can go out on your own." When Maya nods her agreement, I rub my hands together and bounce on my heels. "Now, what should we do?" I need something fun to take my mind off the fact that I'm still not certain about this whole party planning business and that my life might not be coming together as much as I had hoped. "Oh, I know. Is there somewhere we can go karaoke?"

Jake groans and Maya winces slightly, but she nods. "Yes. There's a pub on Main Street that does karaoke on Sunday nights."

"Perfect." I give both of my friends a taunting look. "I don't like to brag," I say, ignoring Jake as he sputters his disagreement with my idea of a good time. "But I'm not a bad singer, so you all better bring your A game."

"Oh, I'm not worried about me," Jake mumbles. I know for a fact that he's not a great singer, so I'm not sure what he's talking about.

Before I can get any clarification, Carter walks over and joins us, turning his head back to the kids before looking at the three of us with wide eyes. "The kids are starting to get a little squirrely, so we might need to move onto something else."

Jumping into hostess mode, I clap my hands to gather all the kids' and adults' attention. "All right, everyone. Who's ready to break a piñata?" The kids squeal, and the adults wince at the loud sounds, but we all move over to the big tree and get ready to watch them get out their toddler aggressions on the newspaper crafted tyrannosaurus.

As we walk, Carter comes up to my side. "This party has been a huge hit." He leans closer and nods at me. "You don't seem as happy about that as I thought you might be." The sound of his low, honeyed voice has me reeling, but it's his words that cause me to nearly trip over my feet. *Busted.*

Carter reaches out to steady me with a hand on my arm. With a fierce blush overtaking my cheeks, I right myself and look up into the deep green sea of his eyes. "You noticed, huh?" When Carter nods, I simply shrug. "I just don't know if it's the right fit, you know? Planning the party for JJ was great, but I'm not sure how good it will feel if I'm doing it for strangers. That seems a lot like the job I just left, and while it wasn't all bad, it wasn't great either."

Carter nods in agreement. "I get it, and luckily you have time to figure it all out." He reaches behind me and pulls me closer to him. "Either way, I'm proud of you for all you did for JJ and for knowing that even though you enjoyed it, it might not be the right fit for you."

Floored by his words, I'm momentarily stunned into silence. "Thank you. That means a lot." It means a lot more than I can express with words, but they're all I have at the moment. Carter nods and continues on toward the piñata area while I'm rooted to the ground, wondering why the words he just spoke to me, the same words that my best friend of just about forever said earlier, somehow mean so much more when they're coming from him.

****

The Ram's Shed Pub is a lot busier than I would have expected for a Sunday evening, but Maya mentioned that summer brings in a lot more tourists and it's not unusual to see crowds this size up until late fall. If I would have known that there would be this many people, I might not have picked karaoke. I'm not worried about myself. Working a crowd has been something I've done and perfected over many years of partying and playing hostess to clients, but I know Carter is a little more reserved and I feel bad that he might feel pressured to get up in front of everyone and sing. The last thing I want to do is ding his confidence when I know that's something he has struggled with in the past.

"Maybe we should go somewhere else," I suggest. The four of us have sat at a table closer to the front of the makeshift karaoke stage and have already placed our drink orders. "We can have a few drinks here and then move on to another spot."

"Oh, ho, no way," Jake argues. He smiles at the waitress as she drops off his beer, wine for me, and two cherry colas for Maya and Carter. The first time I had alcohol in front of the siblings, I felt bad since their parents were killed by a drunk driver. When I said as much, they assured me that just because they choose not to drink doesn't mean they have a problem with other people indulging as long as they do it responsibly. Now I don't feel bad about the occasional glass of wine, but make sure to refrain from even that if I plan on driving. "You wanted to show off your skills, so now you're going to."

My eyes widen and I nonchalantly nod my head in Carter's direction, but Jake just shakes his head at me. "Fine. We can stay," I announce. Reaching over to Carter, I clasp his shoulder. "No one else needs to feel pressured to sing, though."

Carter gives me a funny look. "Okay, but I'm kind of excited to do it. I brought Jake and Maya once a while back, and it's been a long time."

"Not long enough," Jake mutters. Before I can ask him about it, our conversation is interrupted as our waitress comes back and takes our order. In the meantime, a particularly nasally-voiced individual has started singing Miley Cyrus's, "Party in the USA." To their credit, the crowd claps and cheers at the end despite our collective ears having bled for the last three minutes straight.

As I flip through the song catalog, my eyes light up when I find one of my favorite tunes to sing. Scribbling down my choice, I pass it up to the deejay and look over to see Carter writing down his choice as well. "What are you singing?"

Carter holds the paper to his chest. "That's a secret." He smiles and winks before he walks the paper up to the deejay himself.

While my mind reels as it tries to process the sexy

wink I just got, I dumbly turn to the rest of the table. From the looks on their faces, Maya and Jake are still struggling to pick a song. "What are you two going to sing?"

Maya shrugs and Jake looks pained for a moment before a smug smile takes over his face. "Actually, I think we'll sit this one out and leave it to the professional." Maya starts to talk, but he quiets her with a quick kiss on her lips. "No, let her find out the hard way."

"Find out what?" I ask. Before anyone can elaborate, I'm being called to the front for my song. Doing a little shimmy in my chair, I stand and turn to the front, smacking directly into a hard wall of man. From the mossy, wooden smell flowing over me, I can tell it's Carter, and I would love nothing more than to bask in the scent as well as the warmth radiating from his body.

My eyes find his and see that he's smiling sweetly down at me. "Good luck, *Elskling*." He spins me to the front and gives me a gentle shove to the stage. I'm glad of his help because my mind is still stuck on whatever he just called me. I wish I knew what the word was so I could look it up later, but I was too caught up in my fantasies to really be paying attention.

Shaking off my Carter-induced haze, I grab the microphone from the deejay and head onto the stage while the opening notes of Nancy Sinatra's "These Boots are Made for Walking," starts to play. The fact that I am wearing strappy heels and not boots isn't lost on me, but the red shoes paired so much better with my flowy blue skirt and black shirt that I don't even care about authenticity at the moment.

As the beat plays, my body starts to move and I sing the opening lines of the song as I saunter back and forth across the stage. Every now and then I'll stop and do a shimmy, earning a few cat calls from the crowd and

I point out into the audience and wiggle my hips. My voice isn't as great as some other practiced singers, but what I lack in vocal talent I make up for in showmanship. After another minute, the song ends and as the crowd applauds, I pass the mic back, hop down from the stage, and walk victoriously with my head held high back to my table.

Carter claps as I take a seat and slug some water. "Very impressive," he tells me. His eyes are lit up and he does look genuinely impressed, and I find myself sitting a little taller and preening under the attention. It's different from when other guys would be impressed with me because I know Carter better now and can tell he's not as easily awed, and because of who he is, his opinion carries much more weight than any of the other guys I've been with. *You're not with Carter.* The reminder from my brain is unwelcome and dampens my mood slightly.

When the deejay calls Carter's name, I once again feel as though I need to give him an out, especially since he'll have to follow my performance. "You really don't have to sing if you don't want to."

Jake snorts and shakes his head at me with a cheeky expression on his face. My brow furrows at him, but Carter touching my shoulder pulls my attention away from my slightly annoying friend. "I think I'll be all right, but thanks for your concern."

Nodding, I watch as he walks up to the stage. After he grabs the mic, he faces the crowd and a few of them cheer before he's even done anything. "What's that about?" I ask Maya.

"You'll see," she says with a smile. Her attention goes back to her brother as does mine, the opening notes of Chris Isaak's *Wicked Game* starting to play.

"Why would he pick such a difficult song?" I ask myself more than the others. The answer comes as Carter starts to sing, his honeyed voice carrying over the crowd as he hits every note perfectly. "Holy shit." Turning back to look at Maya and Jake, I wince as I see Maya shrug and Jake with an extremely self-satisfied look on his face as he crosses his arms and watches my face grow redder.

Feeling slightly ridiculous for thinking that I was some pro and that Carter wouldn't be able to hold his own, I turn back and watch as he takes command of the stage. His voice easily moves from low and husky to higher and crisp whenever the song calls for it. Every note resonates within me, and as I watch him sing with such power and confidence, my panties practically soak through and I start to squirm in my seat. It doesn't help that he's picked one of the sexiest songs of all time. Each word he sings about falling in love brushes over me like the light whisper of fingertips on skin, causing me to shiver as goosebumps break out all over my body. If he was ever worried about his dates, all he needed to do was forget the small talk and belt out a few notes because I'm ready to jump him right now and the song is only halfway finished.

Once Carter's performance is over, the crowd erupts into raucous applause. He smiles shyly and takes a small bow before handing the mic back to the deejay and coming to the table. When he sits down, he smiles at the plate of food that appeared in his spot while he was on stage being a rock star, exuding sex all over the stage. "Awesome," he says as he picks up his cheeseburger. "I really worked up an appetite."

"Same," I mutter. The appetite I have is not for the pub fare in front of me but for the man on my right. Trying not to drool on myself as I stare at him, my eyes linger on the mouth that just sang so beautifully. "Where the hell did you learn to sing like that?"

Carter's shoulder bounces as he chews his food.

"I did choir in high school," he explains.

Maya rolls her eyes and leans in. "He's being modest," she says with an indulgent glare aimed at her brother. "He's always been a good singer, and the choir won the state competition his junior and senior year with him getting a ribbon for best solo performance. He could have been in All State Choir if he wanted to."

Carter smiles at his sister before turning to me. "It's not that big a deal."

Tell that to the panties that just melted off my body. Leaning in so our dinner companions don't hear, I whisper over to him. "Well, I definitely think we should showcase your skills a little more when we set up your app profile."

Carter shakes his head. "No, I don't want to come off as a braggart."

I snort. "Says the man that just performed like he was born on a stage." He shrugs and I let it drop for now. "Fine, but you should definitely keep that song in your back pocket so you can serenade someone sometime. That is a sure fire way to get the girl."

Carter's eyes bore into mine. It feels like he's seeing something deep down inside me that I myself haven't even found yet. He smiles sweetly at me, and my heart squeezes because it almost hurts to look at something so incredibly beautiful. "I'll remember that."

We go back to eating and talking a little more about what my next party planning gig could be if I decide to go that route, Jake's latest client, and Maya wanting to go full time with her crochet business, but my heart isn't quite in the conversation. It's stuck on the man next to me and wondering what it is he saw that had him smiling like that.

Chapter Eleven

Carter

The week following our impromptu karaoke night is a busy one, so much so that I barely see Billie at all. I've wanted to pull her aside and explore the look I saw in her eyes that night, the look that indicated she might be as interested in me as I am in her, but I haven't had a minute to spare and now it seems like the moment has passed. Even my evenings have been taken up with working on a few extra orders that have poured in. At this rate, we might have to hire another person since Billie and Maya are working more hours than those of a combined full-time employee.

The additional orders coming in are great, but between working on them and also having to help out in the store on occasion, I barely have had time to do anything beyond that besides showering, grabbing a quick meal, and then passing out on my bed only to wake up and do it all over again. Happily, it's Saturday, and once work is done, Billie and I are watching JJ so that Maya and Jake can have a date night before picking him up tomorrow morning. Having a fun night at home with JJ and Billie is just what the doctor ordered after the rough week I've had.

The three of us have big plans to paint, make our own pizzas, and then watch Daniel Tiger's Neighborhood while eating a dessert Billie assures me will taste good even if it looks like baby food to me. It may sound mundane to other people, but it's just the type of evening I would love to have more of. Sitting at home with loved ones, just enjoying each other's company. Thinking of Billie as one of my loved ones doesn't come as a surprise. The more I get to know her, the more I care about her.

Each day that passes has me learning more about the incredible woman she is, and whether she is dominating a karaoke stage in a knock-out dress or curled up in a ball on the couch in sweatpants and a t-shirt while we watch reality television, she's someone I want to be with, and not just as a friend or roommate.

Every time I think I see her feeling the same way, like I thought I did last weekend, she brings up my dating profile and how we need to get it set up. She keeps asking me what the holdup is, but I haven't had the time or the courage to tell her that it's because the only woman I can picture myself being with is her. Clearly she doesn't feel the same way since she is so gung-ho about my dating profile. Maybe it would be best for me to try and forget about Billie and see what else is out there, but I just can't bring myself to do it. It hasn't helped that she's been making dinner all week, passing me a warm plate as soon as I get home so I don't have to do anything other than crash out. How am I supposed to forget about the smart, caring, sexy woman that's right in front of me?

"Smile," I hear over my shoulder. I jump at the intrusion, and when I turn, I see Billie tapping on her phone, likely taking pictures of me.

"Do you have to keep doing that?" It isn't the first time she's popped into the shop for a candid photo to put on the dating app, but it's the first time I've responded in such a sour mood. When her face falls, I immediately feel like a heel and drop my cleaning cloth on the table to go apologize. "I'm sorry," I tell her, reaching up and grabbing both of her shoulders. "It's been a long week and you know I don't love getting snuck up on, especially in here."

Billie nods, looking a little guilty herself. "I know, but I figured you were done since you were cleaning. Besides, you haven't let me take any other photos for your profile, so I've had to resort to busting out my ninja skills."

Nodding, I remove my leather apron and hang it up on the wall. "Tell you what. How about we have fun with JJ tonight, and after he's down we can talk more about the dating profile." I don't love the idea of finally filling it out, but I do enjoy spending time with Billie, and if this is the best way to go about getting more of that, so be it.

"Yay," she exclaims. Her lithe body shimmies and I try to ignore the way my body heats at the movement. It's a skill I have yet to perfect, but I keep trying.

Once we've locked up the workshop and the store, we head up to our apartment to prepare for our incoming guest. After a long shower to wash off the work week, I dress and come out of my room to find that Maya and Jake have already taken off and see JJ playing with the set of blocks I made him a while back. Billie looks over at me from her spot next to our nephew on the floor. "I'm trying to show Little J how to build a fashion runway for his dinosaurs, but he insists on making a fort for them to tear down." She looks back at the boy next to her and ruffles his hair. "Maybe I'll have to take you on a shopping spree like your uncle so that you can appreciate the finer points of the fashion industry."

Crouching down next to them, I give her a wry look as I place another block on the fort. "I don't think I have a deeper appreciation for fashion, though I will admit that wearing clothes that fit is a nice change."

Billie's gaze rakes over my more snugly fitting shirt, her eyes leaving a trail of heat in their wake. "I agree," she says. Her voice is sultry, but she coughs so maybe it was a throat issue. That seems far more likely that her having the hots for me, so I move past it as best I can.

Plopping down next to my nephew, I bump him lightly with my elbow. "So, J. Do you want to keep building a fort, paint, or make pizzas?"

JJ looks thoughtful for a moment before he stands unexpectedly, knocking over his fort as he rushes into the kitchen yelling, "Pizza."

Billie turns to me with laughter in her eyes. "I guess we're doing pizza."

"I'd say so." I stand and reach down to help her up, pulling a little harder than necessary so that she ends up closer to me when she stands. "Sorry about that."

Billie swallows. "No worries." She walks over to the kitchen and I make a concerted effort not to let my eyes linger on the way her pants cling to her firm ass or the way her tank top shows off her full breasts. "Okay, J. What do you want on your pizza? We have mushrooms, olives, peppers…"

"Cheese," he shouts, slapping his hands on the counter.

Billie smiles at him and pats his small hands. "I guess you save all your imagination for your building and not your meals." She opens the fridge and pulls out the sauce and toppings while I start to divvy up the dough we made at lunchtime.

"You're one to talk. What was it you made for dessert, rice pudding? How is rice a dessert?" I tease as I pass a piece of dough for her to roll out.

"Whatever," she says, patting the dough and passing it to JJ. She helps him top it with exactly what he wants, just mozzarella cheese, before putting it on a baking sheet. "You're going to be eating some crow as well after you try it and discover how amazing it is."

An hour later, the three of us are watching Daniel Tiger and learning about food allergies while eating the dessert Billie made. JJ downed it quickly, and while it's not my favorite, the cinnamon does add a nice flavor. As I take another spoonful, Billie looks over at me with a triumphant grin plastered on her face. "So, are you ready for that serving of crow or what?"

Shaking my head, I roll my eyes at her as I eat. "I still stand by what I said about this not being a dessert, but it's not as bad as I thought it would be." I take another bite and hum in pleasure. "I think I'll really start to get into it when I'm ninety and no longer have all my original teeth." Billie grabs a throw pillow and tosses it at my head. It narrowly misses before tumbling to the ground. "Such violence in front of the impressionable youth? I'm appalled."

Billie chuckles and smiles before turning her attention back to the show. Once it's finished and we've gotten JJ all ready for bed, I walk him over to my room but notice Billie hesitating in the doorway. Turning to my nephew, I point at the pile of books I laid out for him near his travel bed. "Why don't you pick out a book to read for me, bud?" He toddles off and does as I ask as I turn my attention to Billie. "What's up?"

She shrugs a shoulder, looking a little self-conscious. "I don't want to make him uncomfortable so close to bedtime." She peers around me and smiles wistfully at him. "He's warming up to me, but I'm not sure he'll be down with me intruding on his routine." Shaking my head at her, I grab her arm and drag her into the room. JJ holds up a *Little Blue Truck* board book and waves it excitedly. I take it from him and smile at the woman next to me. "Would you like Billie to read this to you?"

JJ gets shy all of a sudden, but he nods his head. "Pwease, Biw-ee," he says.

She gasps lightly and clutches her hand to her

chest. "Oh, my god, I think I just ovulated," she whispers. I chuckle as she takes a seat on the edge of the bed and smile when JJ climbs into her lap and snuggles in close. Billie could have anyone eating out of the palm of her hand if she wanted them to, but it seems she's a little more doubtful of herself with the people closest to her. There's no reason for her to be—if anything, we can tell how great she is better than any stranger ever could.

Billie starts to read to JJ as I lean against the wall and watch the two of them, slipping my phone out of my pocket after a minute to snap a few photos to send to her later, knowing how much she'll appreciate it. When she's done, she looks up at me expectantly. "What now?"

Crouching in front of the two of them, I smile up at her but direct my response to JJ. "What do we normally do right before bed, bud?"

"Lullaby," he exclaims happily.

Billie rolls her eyes at me. "I should have known Mister Golden Vocal Cords over here would sing him to sleep," she snarks with a smile. JJ climbs off her lap and into his bed.

As I pull the sheets up and over his small body, I look over at her with a raised brow. "We could always do a duet, you know." I grab JJ's stuffed dog Mr. Buttons and hand it to him. "What do you say?"

Billie leans against the wall, her head slowly moving from side to side. "Thanks, but I think I'll just settle in and watch the show from here."

Shrugging, I turn back to my nephew and sing one of his favorite songs that we've done as a lullaby many times. As I start a slowed down version of "Count on Me" by Bruno Mars, I brush JJ's hair away from his face and gently rub his stomach to help soothe him into sleep. The longer I sing, the heavier his eyelids get and by the time I sing the last note, he's practically asleep. Kissing his forehead, I whisper an 'I love you,' and stand. When I turn to look at Billie, her expression is inscrutable, but she smiles and nods her head at the door.

Once we're outside and out of JJ's earshot, she wanders over to the kitchen and starts cleaning up from our night with the little guy. "You're really good with him," she proclaims as she loads dishes into the dishwasher.

Scooting around the counter to help her, I shoot her a knowing look. "You are too. You just don't give yourself enough credit." Billie is wonderful, but I think she's told herself that she's nothing more than her appearance for so long that she started to believe it. Maybe if I tell her how great she is enough times she'll start to believe that instead.

Her mouth twists. "Maybe not," she says, turning to look at me straight. "But you definitely don't either. Between the woodworking, the singing, and how great you are with Little J, you could have women lining up around the block for you." She points at the phone sticking out of my pocket. "You just need to try."

With a huff, I focus on drying the dishes and not on listening to something I don't want to hear. "I have tried." Not for a long time, and even though I do really want to try again, having Billie in my life has made doing that difficult because when I think about dating, she's the only person that comes to mind.

"Not lately." She stills my hands and tugs on them until I face her once more. Her expression softens and she lightens her tone. "Will you please let me really help you?"

Hearing her beg me to find someone else to date is like a punch in the gut. "Why are you so eager to see me with someone?" A thought occurs to me and I wonder why I hadn't considered it earlier. Billie is much more of a social creature than I am, but she's been spending most of her time with me. "Am I cramping your style or something? You don't have to hang out with me if you don't want to. I mean, if you want to go out around town and meet other people I get it." Heavy emotions clog my throat at the thought of her seeing other guys, but if that's what she wants, I won't stand in her way. At the end of the day, seeing her happy is more important than my silly crush. Even as I think it, I know that what I feel is way more than that, but I' not sure I can face that at the moment.

"Carter," she sighs. She sounds exasperated as she pinches the bridge of her nose. "You aren't cramping my style." When her eyes meet mine, they shine with sincerity. "I meet plenty of new people at the store, but that's not the point. Seeing how great you are with JJ, and knowing that you want that for yourself, well, I just want you to be happy. You should get to have people of your own." She smiles sadly at me and bumps my shoulder. "You can't tell me you don't want that too."

Exhaling slowly, I nod. "I do, but it's been so long and I was never great with women to begin with. If I go out there now after all this time, I'm going to make an even bigger fool of myself than I did years go." The idea of meeting up with strange women and seeing their disappointment has my gut twisting in knots.

"Ugh, Carter," Billie censures. Grabbing my hand, she drags me over to the couch and pulls me to sit next to her. "You are a great guy, but your confidence level sucks. Going out on more dates will help you feel better about your ability to do it."

Scrubbing my hands down my face, I sigh, exasperated with myself. "I know." My head hits the back of the couch and I study the exposed beams on the ceiling before rolling my head to look at her. "How am I supposed to gain confidence from dating when the idea of dating is what is ruining my confidence? It's not like school where I could take a practice test or something. There is no such thing as practice dating."

Billie's expression goes from stern to thoughtful, and a smile tugs at the corner of her mouth. "What if there was though?" As I stare at her in confusion, she rolls her eyes and scoots closer to me. "What if there was a way for you to practice dating?"

If only that were really a thing. "That would be great, but the last time I checked, it doesn't exist." I turn my gaze back to the ceiling, only for it to be pulled back by Billie's fingers on my cheek. Her fingers scratch against my stubble, causing pleasure to zip up my spine. The other part of not dating and being celibate for years is that I'm so touch starved that even the slightest graze of her skin against mine has me clawing at the insides of my skin with need. I want to lean into her touch, but it's gone before I can, though the lingering warmth on my face travels down and into my chest, settling in my heart and setting up base camp. *I'm so fucked.*

As I continue to stare at her, her smile turns coquettish and I wait for the inevitable teasing that she loves to throw at me, but it never comes. "You could practice date me."

I stare blankly for a moment. As soon as the words register, so does the feeling of complete and utter joy that rushes through my body like a group of stampeding elk down Main Street, but there is no way I could have heard her correctly. Either that or she's just being her usual, flirty self. "Yeah, right," I hedge, studying her face for any signs that she's just messing with me.

Billie scoots closer to me, her smile looking far less coy and much more genuine. "I was being serious,

Carter," she confesses. For a moment, I wonder if I fell asleep and this is some wonderful dream, but when I reach down and pinch myself, the pain shooting through my forearm tells me it's very real. "Come on, it's a good idea. You've been such a good friend to me and I've only been here a few weeks. Let me help you like you've helped me." She leans in closer and whispers in my ear. "I promise to make it fun."

That has my brain and my body on high alert, especially my dick who has not had much fun in almost a decade, but it's quickly replaced when a queasy feeling settles in my stomach when I think about having her for a short time only to have to let her go. Being with Billie only as practice for someone else feels wrong, *unnatural*. Unless of course, over the course of our practicing, I can convince her that I could be the right guy for her. Practice makes perfect after all, and anytime I think about the absolute force of a woman next to me, I think we could be pretty perfect together. Billie is so incredible, and if she's willing to help me boost my confidence, who's to say I can't use that newfound appreciation for myself to get her to appreciate me too? Hoping that my plan doesn't backfire, I search her eyes for a moment before the words I know will forever change my life rush past my lips. "Let's do it."

Chapter Twelve

Billie

The words "let's do it" coming out of Carter's plump, juicy lips that are raised just enough in the corner to show a hint of the more devilish side of him have my mind taking a swan dive directly into the gutter as images of the two of us flash through my mind. Carter and me naked together in my bed, his bed, in the shower, and in the workshop all come to the forefront of my brain, though I am sure we would end up with sawdust in places that it never belongs if we actually tried to have sex in the workshop. The longer I think about these scenarios, the more I'm patting myself on the back for the brilliant idea I just presented to him. What I'm thinking must register on my face because Carter's eyes bug wide and a blush creeps up his neck and cheeks.

"Not *do it* do it, but you know, let's do the whole practice dating thing," he blurts. All signs of the devil on his shoulder are gone as the angel takes the reins once more. Now more than ever, I'm determined to see that more playful side of him come out to play and stay out for more than a few seconds. If anyone needs to indulge himself with a little fun, it's Carter, and if I can help him gain enough confidence to go out there and do that a little more often, I'll be happy. Carter has been such a big help to me, it's only natural that I offer up my services in return. *Yeah, sure. That's why you're doing this.* Admitting to anything beyond that isn't something I'm ready to confront just yet, especially since it involves a lot of self-reflection and how even though I'm not sure what direction my life is heading in, I can't help but want to drag the one person who seems to see me for who I really am along for the ride.

Placing that mess of emotions on a shelf to ponder later, I look over at the nervous man next to me. "Great." I shift so that I can face Carter more and smile when he mimics my posture. "First things first. We should list off what you want to practice."

Carter's blush deepens and I make my own list of things to bring up later when he doesn't look like he's about to turn into a literal beetroot. Rubbing the back of his neck, a nervous gesture of his that I find more endearing the more I see it, he dips his head down and peers up at me through unfairly long eyelashes. "I'm not sure. I mean, we could go out to dinner or maybe do a trial run of a real date?"

He looks and sounds so unsure, a bit like a lost puppy that I want to pull him into my chest and keep him safe from others forever. That won't be helpful, though, and even though I know I have my own selfish reasons for doing this that I may or may not examine later, above that, I want to be an actual help to him too. Moving quickly, I grip Carter's strong shoulders and straddle his lap, sitting on his thighs. It would be so easy to slide a little further and just start grinding, but I'm pushing boundaries enough as it is and I don't want to do anything he doesn't want. His eyes stay glued to where my ass meets his legs for a moment before they shoot up to mine, and only then do I speak. "Carter, we have dinner every night, have gone out to eat, and gone out hiking together. You were an active listener and total gentleman the entire time. I don't think us sharing a meal at the local steakhouse is going to give you the confidence boost you need."

Carter nods and licks his lips nervously. "What do you suggest then?" His gaze flicks to my mouth, and that's all the indication I need that he would be on board with what I'm planning. Still, he's so skittish that I have to come at this slowly and carefully, like a lion stalking its prey. When I think about being with Carter, words like devour and ravage are definitely ones that come to mind, but I can't be too forward, not yet.

"What I'm suggesting is that you embrace your Viking heritage a little more." Grabbing and releasing his hands that have been balled up at his sides, I place them on the small of my back and lean in. My own hands drop to his chest, and when his breath hitches then exhales shakily, my stomach flips.

Have I ever had this kind of effect on anyone? Doubtful. The guys I've been with before were basically male versions of me, full of confidence and singularly focused on getting to the good part. Carter looks like he's coming undone at the seams and we've barely even started. What makes it even more unbelievable is knowing that it's not just because he finds me attractive or sexy, but because he likes who I am. In fact, I don't think he's ever openly complimented me on my appearance. It's evident enough in how he looks at me, but him making sure I know how much he appreciates everything else first has me feeling like a half-baked brownie, all warm and gooey inside. Now it's time to return the favor.

"Pillage, plunder, ravage, destroy," I whisper huskily in his ear, grazing his ear with my lips. "I want you to."

His hands tighten on my back and dip lower until they rest on the top of my ass. "What exactly are you telling me?" His breathing quickens and I can feel the evidence of his arousal underneath me. I haven't dry humped anyone since I was a teenager, but suddenly it seems like it's time for a little reminder of how good it can feel.

Leaning back, I leave just enough room so that he

can see into my eyes, see how serious I am when I tell him this. "What I'm saying is, I am giving you permission to use me. Use my body as practice. You know how to make conversation, how to get people to open up. You're social when you want to be, but what you need is a little more practice with the physical side of dating. You need to see how much someone can appreciate your body, for someone to show you that with more than words so that maybe you actually believe them." Running my hands higher and playing with the hair at the nape of his neck, I tip his head back and raise a brow. "What do you say, Viking? Are you game?"

Carter's eyes search mine intently for a moment. "Yes."

The words barely leave his mouth before I press mine against it, sinking into the soft feel of his lips and memorizing the sound of his surprised whimper. Carter stills for a moment, and I panic at the thought of having gone too far too fast or doing something he didn't really want, but then his hands slip to my hips and grip me so tightly I might have bruises tomorrow. *Worth it.* His tongue peeks out sheepishly to lick me, and before he can retreat I suck it into my mouth, swallowing more moans while making some of my own. The kiss is a little unpracticed at first, our noses bumping unceremoniously and teeth clacking a bit, but then our tongues dance together as naturally as if we have been doing this with each other for years, decades even.

We continue to explore each other's mouths while our hands tentatively explore each other's bodies. Well, Carter's are tentative, barely dipping into the tops of my back pockets, but mine are very sure as they slide down his torso and dip under his shirt to feel the happy trail I've gotten to see but not touch as much as I've wanted. As my fingers dance over the light dusting of hair, I smile against his mouth before going back for more kisses. The feeling of absolute rightness that streams through my body is so different than anything I've ever felt before that I get a little light-headed.

Needing air, I slow our kiss and nip at his bottom lip before pulling away completely, sucking in a welcome lungful of oxygen as I look at the man underneath me. Carter's pupils are dark, the black all but crowding out the leafy green I love so much. Our breaths mingle as we gulp down air, coming down from the brief but heavy make-out session that we shared and that I want to repeat, *pronto*. Carter swallows, the sound audible over the quiet of the room. "That was," he exhales slowly, shaking his head. "That was ... well, clearly I don't have words."

Chuckling, I smile and lightly brush my lips against his one last time. "Me either, Viking. Me either." A small shout sounds from Carter's room, and I jump off of him, stumbling to the floor. If I'm not bruised from Carter's grasp, I certainly will be from hitting the hardwood.

Carter leaps up and helps me to my feet. "You all right?" he asks, his eyes looking more normal, though filled with concern.

Nodding, I hike a thumb over my shoulder "I'm good. You can go check on Little J." Carter starts to walk towards his room, but I stop him by grabbing his forearm. When my eyes look down, I see a very large bulge in his pants and make a mental note for later practice sessions. "I'm going to go to bed, but that was just round one, Viking. I hope you're ready for round two soon."

With a wink, I release Carter and head into my own room, throwing open the window to let some of the night air inside. Cooling off from our first practice session is necessary if I'm going to have any hope of sleeping, but if the feeling stirring in my chest when I think about the man I just left are any indication, I might not be getting much sleep anyway.

****

As it turns out, I did get some sleep, though memories of the exploratory kissing Carter and I did made a reappearance in my dreams and may have escalated into something far naughtier than what the two of us did on the couch. When I woke up, I was a sweaty, horny mess and even taking care of business in the shower didn't quench my desire for more. As we sat and had breakfast together this morning, I had to make a real effort to not offer to jump straight to sex. The only thing that stopped me was the presence of our nephew, but even after Jake and Maya took their son back home, I said nothing.

Carter probably isn't ready for that, although he does seem totally unbothered by the whole situation from the night before, so maybe it didn't affect him as much as it did me. He calmly made breakfast in a t-shirt and a pair of sweatpants that clung to him in such a way that had me squirming in my chair at the dining table. Thinking back on it now as I help customers in the store, I can't believe I made it through the morning without crawling over to him, climbing into his lap, and purring like a kitten begging for a dish of milk.

"Are you all right, dear?" the kindly Ms. Heath asks me. I met her earlier this week when she came in to drop off more bars of the handmade soaps she creates at home and sells at the shop. I started using one of her rose-scented milk bars last week and I must say, the woman knows her soap. Even the expensive French soap I'm used to using isn't as good as the one she makes.

Looking over at the middle aged woman, I smile and nod. "I'm good, thanks. I was just a little lost in thought." Lost in a sea of lustful thoughts about the man that is currently working on a bed frame for some guy who owns the ski lodge one town over. When I saw the plans for it on Carter's desk, I almost suggested we quality control test it when he's finished, but he looked so focused on work that I figured I could save that little suggestion for a later date. "How are you today, Carol?"

She smiles as she walks up to the register where I'm stationed and passes over a silver goblet made by another artisan for me to ring up. "I'm well. I just found out that they're going to start having a Sunday farmer's market over in Green Valley, so I might go and see if there are any other soap sellers. If not, maybe I'll set up a stall." She leans in and looks at me conspiratorially. "Don't worry, though. It won't take any business away from the shop."

Smiling, I process her sale and run her credit card. "Well, we appreciate you thinking of us." The farmer's market might be a good place to find more artisans to feature at Hodgepodge, and I try to remember to tell Maya or Carter later on. Their store is doing well, but it could always be doing better. It would also be nice if they didn't have to rely on Carter's creations as much as it seems they have been. He works too hard and needs time for a little more fun in his life.

"Of course," Carol tells me as I hand her the purchase. Her gaze moves over my shoulder to where a picture of Carter, his sister, and their parents hangs in a carved wooden frame. A sad smile comes across her face and she reaches over and pats my hand. "It was just the two of them for so long. It's nice to see that they have more people around to care for them."

My throat goes dry as I absorb her words. I do care about Carter and Maya, and of course Jake and JJ too. But I'm leaving eventually, aren't I? What then? Unable to form words, I simply smile and nod at the woman as she walks out the door.

My gut churns as I think about what I'm doing with my life, or rather, not doing. So far all I have figured out is that I'm not really sure I want to plan parties, I like talking to the people in town, and I *really* like kissing Carter. If only I could turn that into my life's purpose, I would be set. Unfortunately, I need to figure out some kind of direction or I'm never going to leave square one. My phone buzzes under the counter and I grab it quickly, wanting a distraction from unpleasant thoughts about how frivolous my life has been. Unfortunately, the text on my screen from Jake provides no break from my downward spiraling.

Jake: **When did you want to get together to make a business plan?**

Groaning, I type out an excuse to put him off. *Again.* Jake has been asking me about my party planning idea since JJ's birthday, but I haven't had the courage to tell him I changed my mind. Jake has always had his professional life in order, creating and following plans easily since he has essentially been doing it since birth, so it's hard to admit to him that I don't have a plan still. He'll probably lecture me when I eventually come clean, and I'll deal with that when the time comes, but until then, I want to forget about my future and just enjoy what's happening at present.

The back door opens just as I'm putting my phone away and Carter strides in. His hair is damp and his white shirt is a little more translucent from perspiration, but when he stops next to me, he smells as fresh and clean as if he came straight from the shower. Before I can slide down another rabbit hole of dirty thoughts, he starts rubbing the back of his neck, the telltale sign that he's nervous about something. Spearing him with a look, I nudge him with my hip. "All right. Out with it."

Carter doesn't look surprised at my being able to read him, and even though I probably shouldn't be able to after only knowing him for such a short time, it's pretty easy. It's obvious what is going on with him if you take the time to look hard enough, and I do. The fact that no other woman has bothered makes me irrationally angry on his behalf, yet grateful at the same time because it means I get to be the first to appreciate him the way he deserves. *But you won't be the last.*

My brow furrows at my inner monologue, but luckily, Carter speaks and I push the hurtful thought of him with someone else aside. "Well, I know you said that I could talk to people and didn't need that kind of practice, but I was still hoping that maybe we could go out on a date tomorrow night." I hesitate because with the way I'm already feeling about him, going out on an actual date, whether it's practice or not, is dangerous for my heart since he is exactly the type of man anyone could easily fall for. *As if you haven't already.* More unhelpful thoughts, but like the knight in shining armor he is, Carter saves me once more. "If it sweetens the deal, I'll let you pick out my outfit and show me how to style my hair."

The deal didn't need to get any sweeter, but I smile at his willingness to let me play dress up with him. "Done." We shake hands, but instead of releasing them right away, they linger together. The air around us seems to spark and crackle as we continue to touch and stare at one another. I lick my suddenly dry lips and lean up on my toes, but the bell for the shop door ringing has me springing back from him. "It's a date," I tell him. My voice is husky and I cough to clear my throat.

An amused smile plays on Carter's face as he backs away from me. "I look forward to it." Carter nods at the customer who just came in, but his gaze never leaves mine. "See you at lunch." With that, he turns and strides out the door, once again leaving me wondering how I could possibly continue with my plan to help him and protect my heart at the same time.

Chapter Thirteen

Carter

The decision to ask Billie out on the date was easy. If I'm going to convince her to be with me permanently and not just as my dating tutor, we need to spend more time together outside of the apartment, though after the way she straddled my lap and kissed me the other night, having more privacy is also incredibly tempting. Her lips were so smooth and supple, but they moved with such force that it was the very definition of killing me softly. With each pass of her lips, each swipe of her tongue, I fell a little more under her spell. It was a heady feeling that nearly had me floating away if not for the fact that her hands were all over my body, grounding me to Earth with the need to feel every sensation her touch provided. Trembling, shivering, melting and just about any other adjective I could think of to describe what I was feeling were all words that ran through my mind later that night as I thought back on our practice session on the couch. During, my mind was completely blank of anything other than how good it felt to be with her. And how natural.

Being with Billie is as easy as breathing most of the time when I can get out of my head long enough to feel the truth in what she tells me. That I'm a great guy that is worth knowing or that I'm sexy. But in the bright light of day when I'm alone with just my thoughts, it's hard not to pick at what I think are flaws. I can get lost in my work, my sister and nephew are a bigger priority than some women might like, and I lack confidence in myself when it comes to romance. Case in point, I had no idea what to do for a date, and after spending way too much time online searching for "romantic date ideas," I'm still not sure that the fancy restaurant idea I came up with will end up being what I hope it is, a way to slowly convince Billie to stay with me, be with me the way I want to be with her. With a hope that things go well, I step into the bathroom to start getting ready.

The shop closes at 5:00, but I knocked off an hour early to come upstairs. Billie assured me that she had everything in hand and since I would literally be one story above her if she needed anything, I felt comfortable leaving her in charge. She might have had a hard time in the beginning, but after stumbling out of the gate, Billie picked everything up in no time and runs the shop a lot better than I do and is even giving Maya a run for her money. She greets each and every customer from town by name and treats tourists to the area like they are a new friend she just hadn't met yet, showing them around the store and explaining everything in so much detail that I'm constantly blown away by her dedication to a job that is only temporary. I'm really proud of her, though thinking about her situation possibly being short-lived has my stomach sinking.

After a quick shower and changing into the "date night" outfit Billie picked out for me, I'm standing in front of the mirror and trying to remember how I was supposed to put this whole look together. Was I supposed to leave the shirt tucked in or not? And what about the buttons? When Billie had me try this on at the store, I should have been taking notes on how to do it myself instead of floating down the chocolate rivers of her eyes or relishing the feel of her hands on my body as she checked the fit. With a huff, I throw my hands up. Even JJ can put an outfit together, so I'm slightly exasperated with myself for not being able to do something as easy as getting dressed for what could possibly be the most important date of my life.

Moments later, Billie appears in the doorway, a sad smile on her face. "What's the matter?" Her expression shows concern at my distress, but right now the only thing I'm concerned about is not creating a very obvious tent in my slacks. Billie is dressed in a little black dress that shows off shapely legs and toned thighs. As my eyes move higher, they widen at the deep v of the dress that goes almost down to her navel. It doesn't show much, just enough skin and cleavage to get your attention, and boy does it have mine. Trying not to stare like a creep, I look up at her face and see a satisfied look on her face. Clearly, she knows the effect she has on me and doesn't seem at all bothered by it. As she steps towards me, she slowly peruses my body and shakes her head slowly. "I knew I should have left you notes. Clearly you can't be trusted with fine clothes."

Despite her words, I can see the interest in her eyes. The fact that it's there at all has my chest puffing out a bit, pleased that she too likes what she sees. A small laugh escapes my chest as my hands gesture all over my half buttoned dress shirt. "It's not my fault that these buttons are impossible." Billie rolls her eyes at me and I can't help but smile at her. "You're going to have to help me, otherwise I'm going out looking like this and that is as much a reflection of you as it is me."

Billie shakes her head again and comes in front of me, a wry smile on her face. "Low blow going after my ego like that," she says. She shoves the front of my shirt into my pants, which does little to help with my arousal situation, but she's so focused that I'm sure she doesn't notice. "You do a French tuck, so a little in front and none in the back." She opens the top two buttons of my shirt. "And these are open so you look more relaxed." I nod, and when she looks up at my face, she snorts and covers her mouth with her hand. "Sorry. It's just that your hair took me a little by surprise."

Wandering back over to the bathroom, I chuckle when I see my reflection. After using the same goop she did the other day and attempting a style, it turns out I've basically created a look that is very similar to a certain lightning-fast, blue hedgehog. When Billie appears next to me, I smile down at her. "I know I said I would let you do it, but I thought I would give it a go. Clearly, I'm still in need of some tutelage."

She returns my smile as her hands reach up to start fixing my hair. "As awesome as this is, maybe we should save the porcupine quill look for Halloween." Her fingers brushing through my hair feels amazing, and every now and then her nails will graze my scalp and cause a shiver to trail down my spine.

As she continues to adjust my waves, I stare at her, cataloging every feature I can knowing that I'll want to recall them later. Her bronzed skin is so smooth. I want to feel it under the rougher skin of my hands as I cup her face and bring her perfect rose tinted lips up to mine in a kiss. Her eyes are the exact color of my favorite espresso wood stain, a stain I know I'll be using a lot more of from now on just because it will remind me of her. My body sways toward hers without my permission, the same way the wood on my workbench is drawn toward the blade of the saw. Without careful control, the wood will split and I have the feeling if I don't control what I'm doing, I'll be left in one piece, but my heart won't be. Right now, that doesn't seem to matter. "Billie," I whisper.

She hums and looks up at me. The hunger in my gaze must be evident for she waits mere seconds before moving her hands to the back of my neck and pulling me down for another kiss. Our lips crash together like the waves on the shore, but instead of drifting out again, we keep them together, licking into each other's mouths until we're both groaning with pleasure. My hands move into her hair, the strands slipping through my fingers like satin. Billie presses her body to mine, and my back slams into the wall. "Are you okay?" she pants and leans away.

Nodding furiously, I pull her back into my chest and lean down to take her mouth once more. She tastes sweet and spicy, like chocolate and cayenne pepper as I move my tongue against hers, the smooth glide causing the rest of my body to respond fervently. A jolt of pleasure shoots up and down my spine, and my hands travel down to the curve of her ass, lightly squeezing the firm globes and pulling her against the erection that's resulted from each and every one of her touches. Billie whimpers and I swallow it down with a smile. The fact that I can reduce this fantastic woman to whimpers has me feeling like king of the mountain, though I know it's as much her as it is me.

When I squeeze her again, she breaks the kiss, both of our chests heaving with the effort to catch our breath. "What about the date?"

Fuck the date, my dick cries as it literally weeps in my slacks, but if this is going to be about more than just her helping me out, we need to do more than just paw at each other in the bathroom, even though right now that's all I seem to want to do. "Right," I breathe out. Leaning my head back against the wall, I take a few calming breaths and try to will my dick to go down, though it's taking its sweet time. "We should get going."

Billie nods as she catches her breath. "Totally." Turning, she looks in the mirror, her jaw dropping at the sight in front of her. Her lipstick is smeared and her hair is mussed from my putting my hands through it. Her eyes flick to my reflection. "I might need a minute."

Ripping off some toilet paper to wipe the lipstick from my mouth, I clear my throat and head to the door.

"Take your time. I've got my own issues to deal with," I tell her with a wink. Adjusting my pants, I exit the bathroom and make my way over to the door.

"Not cool, Carter," she calls over. As she shuts the door, I smile, enjoying that I'm not the only one twisted up in knots after the kissing.

As I wait for her to get ready, a roll of thunder sounds outside and I walk over to the window just in time to see lightning crash in the near distance. Moments later the sky opens up and starts to pour rain down in sheets. Afternoon and evening thunderstorms are common in the summer, but there were none in the forecast for this evening. "So much for a nice night out." We can still go to the restaurant, but as the rain keeps coming down in buckets and I watch the sides of the street quickly flood with water, the idea of heading out in the inclement weather sounds less and less appealing.

Billie's arm brushes up against mine as she stares out the window. "Oh, no," she says with absolutely zero regret or remorse in her voice. "Looks like we have to cancel our date and stay in. However will we pass the time?"

When I look down at her, her eyes are hooded and she slowly licks her lips. As tempting as it is to go back to making out, I really want this to be more than that. "Just because we aren't going out in that," I tell her, tipping my head out the window. "Doesn't mean our date is canceled." Billie's brow furrows with confusion, and I don't bother resisting the need to smooth it out with my thumb. "No need to worry, *Elskling*. I've got an idea."

Walking over to the kitchen, I smile at my second use of the Norwegian term for sweetheart. It's something I heard my dad use often when he spoke to my mother, and even though I'm not fluent in his native language, I know a few key words and calling Billie my sweetheart just feels right. Billie follows, her heels clacking on the hardwood as I root around the refrigerator, smiling at the ingredients I see inside. Pulling out everything I need to make an easy yet romantic dish, I place it all on the counter and shoot a grin over to the woman next to me. "You can keep me company while I make us dinner."

Billie narrows her eyes at me briefly before she's kicking off her heels and hopping up on the counter, her long, sculpted legs dangling in front of me like a red flag in front of a bull. My body is ready to charge right in, but I will myself to focus on feeding her. "I'm never one to turn down food," she says. Her eyes find mine and she smiles seductively. "But if you're making dinner, that means I'm in charge of dessert."

Swallowing thickly, I try to focus on the task ahead of me and not on what she just said. "Sounds good." My voice cracks slightly and a knowing laugh comes from her lungs. The rich, husky sound is so welcome that I don't even feel embarrassed about my reaction. She knows how inexperienced and nervous I am, but she wants to help me anyway. All I can do at that is smile and hope that after all this, maybe she'll see me not as a project, but as someone who can be a partner for her. That's what I want, and that's what she deserves.

Chapter Fourteen

Billie

Watching Carter adeptly handle himself in the kitchen has easily become one of my new favorite pastimes over the last month or so, and tonight is no different. Carter rolling up his shirt sleeves and exposing the sturdy muscles of his forearms was like a torturous form of foreplay. Then his strong, capable hands made quick work of preparing the chicken before he moved onto making some type of fancy garlic bread, and all I could think about was how he could put his hands to much better use by exploring my body. Even with all that yumminess on display, the best part was that before he even started, Carter poured me some wine, knowing how much I like to relax with a glass of my favorite merlot. The fruity bouquet was a welcome treat, and the dry texture contrasted nicely to the fact that my mouth would water every time the muscles in Carter's forearms flexed as he cut, chopped, and minced, but his thoughtfulness was what affected me most, warming my heart more than the alcohol ever could.

Carter peeks at me out of the corner of my eye as he puts the pan of caprese garlic bread into the oven to broil. "What are you thinking about over there?" He raises a brow, making him look impossibly sexy. I wanted to be good and get through this date without derailing his plans, but it's so hard when he looks at me like that.

"Are you sure you want to know?" I counter. When he nods, I hold out my hand and drag him over to me, pulling him in between my legs. His eyes go from light to dark in moments as his hands rest on the curve at my waist. The fact that he didn't hesitate to touch me feels like a win, but I'll save the victory dance for later. Right now, I want to focus on the incredibly thoughtful and unwittingly sensual man in front of me. Draping my arms over his shoulders, I lean in closer, staring into his forest green eyes. "I was thinking about how considerate you are, and how that coupled with the way you move in the kitchen has me thinking all kinds of ways to thank you properly after dinner."

"Yeah?" he asks, his voice soft. "And what did you come up with?" His gaze moves all over my face but settles on my lips, his tongue peeking out to wet his own.

A wicked smile pulls at the corners of my mouth before I press my lips firmly to his, and he immediately groans and pulls me closer to him. A surprised gasp leaves my mouth, and Carter takes advantage of that by pushing his tongue inside, the naturally spicy taste of him engulfing my mouth in seconds. As we continue to devour one another, our hands start to roam. Mine to the strong muscles of his back and his to the tops of my thighs, his fingers teasing at the hem of my dress. My skin tingles and I squirm a little on the counter, a pressure building between my legs. Every brush of his skin against mine feels amazing, and I can't help but smile a little as the Viking that's been hiding inside of him all along comes out to play for a little bit. Shy Carter is endearing, but Viking Carter is a force all its own, and I am definitely caught up in his thrall.

Just as his fingers skate under my dress, the oven timer sounds and interrupts a kitchen make-out session that I will forever remember as one of my favorites of all time. Carter isn't the most technically skillful kisser I have ever been with, but he is the best in more ways than one. His earnestness and desire to make you feel good above all else is what earns top marks. As we break apart, he smiles hesitantly before getting half our dinner from the oven. Shy Carter is back, but I have a feeling that the Viking isn't as buried as he once was.

"You hungry?" he calls over his shoulder as he plates the chicken piccata and garlic bread.

"Famished," I breathe out. Watching his perky ass move as he carries our plates is impossible not to do, and I give myself a mental pat on the back when I manage not to stumble on my way to the table. Placing his water glass in front of him, I take a seat on the side and dig into the meal, moaning my pleasure as the different flavors hit my tongue. "This is so good."

Carter watches me eat for a full minute before he addresses my comment. "I'm glad you like it," he finally says, taking a bite of his own food. "I love cooking for other people, especially when they seem to appreciate it as much as you do." He winks at me and starts back into his food. After a few moments of comfortable silence and eating, he washes his food down with some water and stares intently at me. "Have you given any more thought to the party planning business?"

"Ugh," I whine, dropping my fork on my already nearly empty plate. Everything tasted amazing and apparently I was hungrier for food than I originally thought. "Jake keeps asking me the same thing and I keep putting him off because I don't know what to tell him. He's my best friend and I don't want to disappoint him."

Carter reaches over and gives my hand a reassuring squeeze. "Let's forget about Jake for the moment and focus on you. That's what you being here is all about anyway, right?"

Nodding, I take a sip of wine. "It is, but he's always had a plan for everything and it feels like he'll be upset with me if I tell him I still don't know what I want to do."

"Plan for everything, huh?" Carter asks, giving

me a wry look. "And how did that work out for him a few years ago?"

"Touché," I admit. Jake's strict adherence to his life plan is what caused him to lose so much time with Maya and his son, and he vowed to be better. I guess that coaxing me into getting a life plan figured out doesn't count. "But even if plans aren't always what they're cracked up to be, it still feels like I should have one by now."

Carter leans back in his chair and shakes his head at me, but there's no censure in his look, only amusement. "Billie, you've been here for what, a month? I think you can cut yourself a little slack. Not everyone has a life plan at the age of seventeen like he did."

"You did," I argue. Carter has told me that he always knew what he wanted to do from the moment his dad showed him how to work with wood. Between him, Jake, and Maya, it seems like I'm the only one who has no idea what they're doing with their life.

Carter shakes his head and scoots closer to me, taking my hand in his once more. "My dad showed me what he loved, and I was lucky enough to love it too. Same with Maya and my mom, but even then, she wants to be an artisan herself more than she wants to discover them for the shop now." Maya has been turning a lot more of the day to day duties at the store over to me so she can focus on her crocheting and all the orders that have been pouring in from her online store. "And you told me Jake basically had a day planner in his hand from birth onward, so you can't really compare yourself to him. You shouldn't compare yourself to anyone else really. You're your own person, no one else matters."

Blinking over at the man next to me, I hide my shaky smile behind my wine glass. "How did you get so wise?" I ask. Swallowing down the last of my drink, I wash down the bitterness I was feeling toward myself as well.

Carter shrugs a shoulder and smiles at me. "I guess all work and no play makes Carter smarter than he looks, but don't change the subject." *Damn.* For a moment I thought he was going to let me get away with not talking about myself, but no such luck. His gaze turns thoughtful for a moment as he peers over at me. "You haven't told me much about how you grew up. Maybe that has something to do with how you're feeling now."

"Maybe." I consider my childhood for a moment and wonder if what Carter is saying has some truth to it. "Well, I grew up in a nice neighborhood and my parents were always very loving, but they also kind of let me do whatever I wanted. It was basically a free-for-all until dinnertime and as long as I got most of my homework done, they didn't care about much else as long as I was happy, at least until high school when I started getting a little too unfettered with the freedom they allowed me. Then it seemed like I was doing stupid things like throwing parties or trashing the rival school's gym just because I could and everyone kind of expected me to."

Carter nods, processing my words. "Maybe it was too much freedom. We all figure out who we are eventually, but when we're little, it's our parents and the adults around us who guide us towards that."

"My parents love me," I tell him adamantly. They do, and maybe they weren't always perfect, but Lord knows neither was I. There were plenty of ways I caused them worry. Even now my dad seems regretful at the fact that I was so lost and worries that I won't find my way back to myself. Whatever that means.

Carter holds up his hands in surrender. "I know they do. How could they not?" Before I can decipher what that last question meant he barrels ahead. "All I am saying is that maybe in an effort to let you be your own person, they forgot that they needed to help you figure it out along the way."

I hit the back of the chair as I take in his words. "Oh." Carter might be right. I kind of always just floated along, doing whatever anyone else wanted me to do with no one showing me the type of person I could be.

Cater hums thoughtfully at my reply, but doesn't utter a word. Instead, he stands up and clears our plates, depositing them into the sink. When he comes back to the table he stops by my chair and holds a hand out for me, pulling me to my feet after I place my hand in his. "Come with me," he commands as he pulls me into the bathroom again.

"If we're coming in here to make out some more, I can tell you right now I am one hundred percent on board with that plan." It will be a little jarring going from talking about my childhood to kissing Carter, but I'm willing to deal with a little cognitive dissonance if it means I get to feel his lips on mine.

Carter chuckles and shakes his head as he positions me in front of the mirror. "What do you see when you look in the mirror?"

Giving myself a long hard look, I see what I normally do whenever I get ready in the morning, with the possible exception that I look a lot more rested than I used to. Shrugging, I turn my eyes to the man beside me. "I don't know what I'm supposed to see."

"Would it help you if I told you what I saw?" When I nod, he gently turns me back to face the mirror, his hands resting lightly on my shoulders. "What I see is a smart, thoughtful, caring, captivating woman who works hard and does whatever she can to make other people happy." He leans over until his head is nearly resting against mine. "I see someone who doesn't have to think too hard about who she is or what she wants to do because right now, the person you are, the person staring back at me, is enough. You are enough, Billie."

Moisture gathers in my eyes at what are perhaps the kindest and most impactful words anyone has ever said to me. Thinking that I am enough just as I am, that I don't need to have a life plan or have everything figured out at the moment has my chest feeling tight, even as all the pressure I had put on myself to have it all together starts to dissipate. Uncomfortable with all this emotion, and the fact that I can tell I've just fallen a little bit in love with Carter, I try to make a joke to lighten the mood. "So what you're saying is I can be whatever I want to be. Even an astronaut?"

Carter rolls his eyes indulgently at me and huffs a laugh. "While I have no doubt that a charismatic person such as you could easily talk their way aboard a spacecraft, that's not what I meant and you know it," he chastises, spearing me with a look in the mirror.

"I know." Reaching up and grasping the hands that rest on my shoulders, I give them a gentle squeeze. "And thank you. I appreciate what you just said. It means a lot."

"You're welcome." His mirror gaze finds mine, and even from here I can tell that his mind has taken a wicked turn. "Now, I think I remember someone saying something about dessert."

Spinning, I pin him to the wall and push my body up against his. "Come on, Viking. Time for something sweet." When I reach up to kiss him, it feels so right that I nearly stumble, but Carter catches me, gripping my arms and holding onto me so tightly I'm not sure he'll ever let me go. More than that, I'm not sure I want him to.

Chapter Fifteen

Carter

The last few days with Billie have been some of the best of my life, and not just because we've been "practicing" kissing every night after work, though that has also been a really great addition to my routine. They've been so great because with each interaction, whether it's a quick hello while I drop some pieces off in the shop or a longer conversation over dinner and some reality television, I get the sense that the two of us belong together. From the moment I saw Billie, something about her drew me in, and the more I get to know her, I realize that it was all of the wonderful qualities she possesses and shows to the world. Because of her stunning beauty, it's easy to see why some people never got past that to see the woman underneath the looks, which is a shame because she is so much more than her appearance. Luckily for me, I seem to be the first one to look deep enough to see it, though it should be obvious to anyone who interacts with her even for a moment.

Anytime I walk into the shop, Billie is either working diligently on making each display look as eye-catching as possible, or she is giving each and every customer her closest personal attention. She treats everyone who enters Hodgepodge with courtesy and kindness, as well as if they were her newest personal shopping client. The other day I walked into the store and she was showing Old Man Lewis a display of scented candles, telling him how if he really wanted to spice up his love life, he needed to create the perfect atmosphere for his lady friend. I didn't even know he had much of a love life, but after only spending a few minutes with him, Billie had gotten him to spill the beans and helped him solve his problem. Seeing as how Mr. Lewis and Ms. Heath were seen canoodling outside on a park bench the very next day, I would say she was successful. If only she could see herself the way I do. She might not yet, but she will if I have anything to say about it.

As I finish polishing the small side project I've been working on this week, I smile when I think of the look that will be on Billie's face when I give it to her. Her gratitude is always evident in her expression, but more than that, it is sincere, which I appreciate. I'm sure she's been given quite a few expensive gifts in her lifetime. Hell, she flew home on a private jet last year. Still, I know that she'll accept my gift with a graciousness that she would display whether I gave her a diamond tennis bracelet or simply made her a ham sandwich.

Shucking my leather apron, I wash up quickly, trying to make myself look as presentable as possible when I've been spending most of my day in the workshop and head over to Hodgepodge. As I enter through the back, my steps slow as I listen to Billie speaking with a customer.

"I can assure you, Janeel. These sea glass earrings would pair well with just about anything, but especially the royal blue dress that's displayed in the window of Nina's Clothing Shop across the street." Billie points out the window and over to another store before turning back to her customer. "Trust me, with these earrings and that dress, your wife will be begging you to skip the anniversary dinner and head straight into the bedroom."

I stifle a chuckle as I watch the middle-aged woman blush, but she nods and takes the earrings over to the counter. As Billie rings her up, she tells her a little more about the origin of the jewelry and offers her some advice about what shoes would go best with the dress I'm sure she's just convinced the other woman to buy.

Finally, when the store is empty, I make my way to the register, smiling at Billie when she turns to me with an excited look on her face. "Hey, this is a nice surprise." She looks me up and down, the look in her eyes making me feel about ten degrees hotter than I had moments ago. "A *very* nice surprise."

Still not used to her attention and compliments, I can feel a blush creeping up my neck and change the subject before I can get too embarrassed. "Speaking of surprises…" I take my project from behind my back and present it to her. "This is for you."

Billie takes the small rose I hand-carved from balsa wood and twists it in her delicate fingers. When she looks up from the gift and into my eyes, I can see them shining with thanks and maybe a little bit of affection. Hoping that affection can turn into something more akin to love, I smile at the look of wonder on her face, hoping it was a good first step toward that. "This is beautiful, Carter." She holds it closer to her chest, a beatific expression on her face. "I love it. Thank you."

"You're welcome," I tell her. As I tuck a loose strand of her dark chocolate hair behind her ear, my fingers brush against the smooth skin of her neck, and I smile as I feel it turn to gooseflesh. She blinks up at me, her eyes soft and filled with tenderness. She looks so peaceful, but she also looks so completely gorgeous, so totally *mine* that I can't not kiss her.

Leaning down, I brush my lips lightly against hers, the softness filling my heart with a peaceful feeling I haven't experienced in quite some time. Billie's hand rests lightly on my chest, and her touch sends my body alight. I'm trying to keep the kiss chaste since we are in the middle of the store, but it's difficult. Clearly, Billie feels the same way because soon she's placing her rose on the counter and shoving me towards the office. "We need some privacy," she announces as she pushes me down into the office chair.

"What about customers?" My body is screaming at me to shut the fuck up, but being responsible is so engrained in me that my mouth is running away with itself.

Billie leaves the office door ajar a few inches. "There." She walks over to me and proceeds to straddle my lap. "Now we'll be able to hear anyone come in."

Feeling her body shift on top of mine and the warmth from her skin has me harder than an iron bar. My blood is definitely not flowing towards my brain, so I'm not quite as confident in my ability to listen for people in the store as she is. "I think you're overestimating my ability to multitask," I tell her. My hands slip down to her cut-off covered ass as I pull her closer to me. When she feels my hardness beneath her, she whimpers and presses against it. It's too much and not enough, and I can't be sure I won't come in my pants from this alone. It's been a long time and Billie feels *really* good.

Billie grinds against me some more, and I groan as the electric feel of it nearly jolts me from my seat. "I can be the eyes and ears for both of us," she breathes out. Expecting her to kiss me, I'm caught off guard when she dives to the side and starts to nibble on my ear. Shivering at the surprise sensations it's causing, I buck my hips up into her, needing more friction. "Oh, you like this, don't you?" A strangled sound leaves my throat as she trails her lips up and down my neck, her fingers twisting in my hair. The small sting from her grip is just about the only thing keeping me grounded as the rest of me threatens to drift away into a sea of gratification. When she reaches the junction of my neck and shoulder, she pulls my shirt to the side and starts to lick and suck at the skin there.

The soft feel of her mouth against me has me

picturing it other, far more sensitive places. "Fuck," I grit out. My mind tries to conjure up unsexy images to keep myself from exploding in my jeans, but it's practically impossible with the most tantalizing woman alive smashing her body against mine.

Billie pops off my neck where I am sure there is bound to be a bruise and smiles wickedly at me. "We're working our way up to that," she confesses, a wicked smile on her face. When she offered to help me "practice dating" I wasn't sure it would go that far, though I can't say I didn't dream it might. "Now where was I?"

Before Billie can start marking me again, the bell above the shop jungles and I hear a voice call out. "Billie? Where are you?"

Billie's eyes widen in panic at the sound of her best friend's voice. "Oh, shit," she exclaims. Her body nearly falls onto the floor when she scrambles off of me.

The horrified expression on Billie's face at almost being caught paired with Jake's continued talking has erased just about every bit of my arousal. Standing, I adjust myself and straighten my shirt. Not liking the stricken look on her face, I try to lighten the mood. "It's just Jake," I tell her, running my hands through my hair. "It's not like we got busted by your parents."

The joke falls flat as Billie tries to right herself. "This is worse than getting busted by my parents." She quickly smooths her hands over her shorts and t-shirt. "Jake would definitely not approve of this."

Hearing that feels like a punch to the gut. Whether he wouldn't approve because he thinks I'm not right for her or good enough doesn't hurt, but her reaction to his presence and the thought that she might agree with him makes me feel a little sick to my stomach. "I guess I'm probably not the type of guy he could see you with." Maybe I'm wasting my time and will eventually get my heart broken, but as I look at the woman next to me, I can't help but think it's worth taking the chance.

Billie's eyes are sad as she looks at me, but at least there is no trace of pity there. I couldn't take it if she was doing this out of pity. "Carter," she starts, but Jake's insistent calling cuts her off. "We're not done talking about this." She opens the office door and smiles over at her friend. "Hey. Sorry it took a minute. Carter was showing me how to update the finances."

The lie came out smoothly enough, but Jake looks between the two of us skeptically. "I didn't think that was part of your duties." He continues to give us a once over, and I hope he misses any signs of what we were up to. I'm happy to declare it from the rooftops, but based on Billie's reaction, she'd rather keep our activities private.

"It's not, but I figured it couldn't hurt to show her a few extra things." I'm a little surprised and pleased with how well the small fib rolls off my tongue. Lying isn't something I do often, but if it will protect Billie from her big, bad best friend, I'll do it.

Jake frowns. "What about your business plan? Don't think I can't tell that you keep blowing me off." He spears her with a look and I watch as Billie shrinks into herself slightly. It's barely noticeable, but it's enough to have me feeling defensive on her behalf.

Rising up to my full height, which is still a few inches shorter than Jake, I step closer to Billie and give him a pointed look. "There's no timeline here. She can take as long as she wants to figure out what her next move is."

Jake gives me a wan look. "Yes, except money is finite and sometimes you have to strike while the iron is hot. Right now, the people she worked with in Denver will be good contacts for her party planning. If she waits, those will dry up and it will be harder to get her business

159

off the ground once she moves back to the city."

Hearing any words about her moving away has my hackles up, and I cross my arms over my chest to try and make myself a little more intimidating even though Jake is clearly more built than I am. "Maybe Billie doesn't want to move back to Denver," I challenge. Jake's eyes narrow at me, but before he can speak again, Billie beats him to it.

"Maybe Billie doesn't like all this male posturing and can speak for herself." She looks at the two of us, her expression defiant as her gaze moves back and forth.

Feeling like a jerk, I shove my hands in my pockets and offer a contrite look. "Sorry," I tell her. One look at Jake tells me he isn't going anywhere, and there is no way I'm going to make myself the third wheel, so I nod at the two of them and step back. "I'll give you two some privacy."

A semi-heated conversation starts to take place, but I can't make out the words as I beat a hasty exit. The warm weather on the walk back to the shop does nothing to help cool me down from both the heated exchange Billie and I shared in the office and the one I had with Jake outside of it. Jake is a great guy, and I know Billie respects his opinion, but it seems like she puts a little too much stock in how he and other people see her when she's already the most amazing person I've ever met. As I cross the threshold into my workshop, my steps falter as I repeat the words back to myself in my head. The exact words I just thought are what Billie has been trying to tell me. I'm already great, I just need to see it and believe it myself. With her help, I've started to, and with a little luck, maybe I can be that same source of assurance for her that she's been for me.

Smiling at the thought, I start to arrange my tools for another rocking chair order when I hear the door to the shop creak open. When I glance over my shoulder, I see Billie walking in with a sad smile on her face. "Sorry about that," she says, hiking a thumb over her shoulder. She comes over and sits on the bench where my tools are spread out. Picking up a pair of small bandy clamps, she raises a brow at me. "Kinky."

"What can I say, I have hidden depths," I say wryly. Taking them from her hand, I set them back on the counter. "And there's no need to apologize. I'm the one who should be sorry. I just know how hard you've been working at the store while trying to figure things out. Seeing Jake push you even harder to make a plan got me a little irritated."

Billie holds out her hand and drags me over to her. "I don't like it either, but that's how he is. Though, I did finally tell him I'm not on board with the party planning anymore." A slow exhale from her lungs brushes over my skin. "He took it surprisingly well." A sly smile plays at the corners of her mouth. "I think he was afraid that I might call my bodyguard back to protect me."

Her arms wrap around my neck and I chuckle at the thought that I would need to protect this fierce woman from anything. "I think you've shown that you are more than capable of handling yourself. I guess I just forgot that for a minute."

Billie shrugs. "Unnecessary though it was, it was actually kind of hot. Maybe next time the two of you could wrestle shirtless or something." Her smile brightens. "Oh, there could be some kind of oil involved too."

Pinching her side, I give her a mock stern look. "Only happening if you're the one I'm wrestling." Leaning down, I brush my lips against hers, keeping it light since technically we're both still at work. Pulling back, I cup her cheek, running my thumb across her skin one last time before stepping back. "Who's running the shop?"

She smiles and pulls me back to her. "I put the 'back in ten' sign up before I walked over here." Her hands dance up the back of my shirt before making their way into my hair. "Time to make use of our last remaining minutes."

As she leans up and takes my mouth with hers, I know that I will try everything I can to be able to keep her. I may not have felt worthy of such a person in the past, but I'll be damned if I let my own doubts get in the way of having the kind of future I can see with Billie.

Chapter Sixteen

Billie

After the long and surprisingly eventful day at the store yesterday, today has been a breeze. Even though it's a Saturday and the shop has been constantly flooded with tourists enjoying spending summer in the mountains, it hasn't been nearly as complicated as yesterday was. Making out with Carter is getting increasingly confusing. I told him I would help him practice dating, but it's starting to feel a lot less like practice and whole lot more like the real thing, especially when he presents me with such beautiful things like the sculpted rose he must have spent a good chunk of time working on. The petals and leaves were so intricately carved that if I didn't know any better, I would mistake it for the real thing. The fact that he spent his time on something like that for me had a warm, tingly feeling spreading all through my body, and when he handed it to me, I wanted to do a lot more than show my thanks with our little grinding session in the office. Too bad the whole effect was ruined the moment Jake spotted my gift on the counter.

As soon as Carter left the two of us alone, Jake pounced. "What is this?" he asked, reaching for the rose. Luckily, I snatched it before he could take it from me. The warning look in his eyes was enough to tell me he knew who it was from. "Billie. I told you not to mess with him."

"I'm not," I had insisted. "Carter wanted to do something nice for me, so he did. That's all this is." The lie felt sour on my tongue the second I uttered it. Not only was I denying that there was nothing more to the rose when I knew it was something significant, but I was denying my own growing feelings for the man that gave it to me.

"Is he why you're dragging your feet on the business plan?" Jake asked. A chastising remark was on the tip of my tongue, but it disappeared at the heavy look on his face. "I'm just concerned about my best friend." Finally fed up with hiding from him, I let him know that I wasn't really interested in party planning anymore, and after thanking him for his concern but telling him it wasn't necessary, I was able to rush him out of the store.

After the confrontation with Jake, there was only one way to improve my mood, so it was no surprise that I found myself in the workshop, pulling Carter close to me, hoping his kisses would help erase the memory of my little spat with Jake from my mind. It worked, for the most part. Last night when I was trying to go to sleep, the memory crept back in as did the thoughts that I wasn't doing enough to get my act together. Though the longer I stay with Carter and worked in the store, the less it seems like my life is spiraling. In fact, the only time I have ever felt that recently was when someone else brought it up or I felt like I should be working toward something else instead of simply enjoying what I was already doing. Surely I couldn't stay here and work in the shop forever, right?

"You're either thinking awfully hard about something or you're extremely constipated," Carter remarked as he stepped into the store. The late afternoon sun streaming through the front window indicated it was almost time to close up, but that didn't register right away. What did register was how good the man in front of me looked, his face glowing and the occasional caramel-colored strand of his hair highlighted from the sun's golden rays. His eyes also struck me as they looked lighter than I have ever seen them, and he carried himself with a lot more confidence than he did even a few days ago.

Finally, his words hit me and I frowned. "Ew. I'm not constipated, nor would that be something we talked about anyway."

Carter shrugged and leaned against the counter next to us. "Sorry. I probably spent too much time talking about the contents of JJ's diapers to remember what isn't allowed in polite conversation." He nudges me with his elbow, his eyes searching mine. "So what were you thinking about?"

Not ready to confront the increasingly complex feelings I have towards Carter, I tell him a half-truth. "Still trying to figure out what I'm doing as far as the old career is concerned."

Carter nods sagely. "Pretty heavy stuff," he tells me. His expression turns thoughtful and he smiles at me. "You need a camping trip." Before I can respond to that, he walks over to the sign on the door and flips it over before locking up.

Checking my watch, I gape over at him as he strides back to me. "We don't close for another hour. We can't lock up now," I rebuke. From the determined look in his eye, Carter's not giving in to my demand.

He shrugs again and pulls me along by my hand. "Owner's prerogative." He smiles over his shoulder at me and winks. The sexy wink as well as the feel of his hot skin against mine has me wanting to forget whatever camping idea he's thinking about and steer him over to my bedroom, or his room, or the couch. Honestly, at this point the sexual tension is so thick between the two of us that I would do it on the floor, bruised knees be damned. "Come on. We're going on a little trip."

Remembering his words from moments ago, I start to drag my feet as we climb the stairs to the apartment. "No way. A hike is one thing, but camping is another. I don't camp." One time I went glamping with some friends and even that was a stretch for me. The accommodations were gorgeous, but we were still out in nature and I had a hard time sleeping without my custom head pillow and white noise machine. I may be a bit of a pampered princess, but it's what I need to get a decent night's sleep.

Carter stops at the apartment door and smiles at me. "I bet I could get you to like camping," he declares. Pushing open the door, he holds it open for me before stepping inside. "I already have a tent and pack ready to go. We can do a quick overnight and be back in the morning." He gives my hand another squeeze and smiles sweetly at me. "Please? It will help clear your mind. I promise."

Spending any time with Carter always sounds like a good idea, and even though being near him all night won't clear my mind of my complex thoughts and feelings, I can't say no to him. "Fine," I announce. Heading into my room to change into more camping appropriate attire, I stop and give him a look. "But if I can't sleep, you have to make soft whooshing noises to help relax me."

Carter walks over and tips my head up to his before his lips bestow a feather light kiss on mine. "I promise to do whatever you need me to in order to help you sleep." He smiles mischievously before heading into his own room, leaving me to wonder exactly what I could ask of him that he wouldn't give me. Probably nothing. That's how selfless he is. The real question is, can I keep myself from being selfish with him?

****

A few hours and one long hike later that Carter assured me would be worth the blisters I am liable to get from my worn out boots, we come to a clearing in the woods next to a beautiful overlook. The sun is just starting to set, and the sky is painted a beautiful pink and purple. Stepping closer to the edge, I look out over Starlight Lake, smiling as I recognize some of the landmarks from the town even in the dimming light. The square with the wishing fountain is visible, as is Main Street. "I wish I had a pair of binoculars so I could see Hodgepodge."

Carter drops his pack on the ground and comes next to me. He squints out at the town and points to a small strip of turquoise that I recognize as the awning that hangs over the storefront. "Right there," he announces. He brushes his lips against my cheek, and when I turn to him he has a big grin on his face. "Who needs binoculars when you have me?"

"You do come in pretty handy," I confess. *In more ways than one.* Carter has not only been helping me figure out what I want to do with my life, but he's helped me figure out who I am, or rather, he's helped me start to see that I was already everything I ever needed to be, I just buried myself under other people's expectations and got a little lost. As I join him in the clearing and drop my backpack, I look over to watch him set up the tent, smiling when I notice there's just the one. "Only one tent, huh?"

Carter blushes slightly and busies himself with the poles and canvas. "I didn't think you'd want to be weighed down by carrying another." His eyes meet mine and they turn serious. "I can sleep outside if sharing makes you uncomfortable."

While I have no doubt that Carter would indeed rough it in a sleeping bag outside if I asked him to, there is no way I am going to do that. "I'm good." Smiling, I grab my phone from my pack and walk over to the view to snap a couple of photos. Turning, I take a few of the man in front of me, wanting to capture as many memories of this as I can. I'll send the one of the view to my parents, but the one of Carter kneeling on the ground, his muscles and round ass on display is just for me. When he catches me snapping photos, he shakes his head, though there is definitely a playful smile on his face. "What? You love the attention," I sass, snapping another picture of his butt for good measure.

Carter makes a few adjustments to the canvas and in seconds, the tent is ready to go. Glancing over at me, he nods. "I do like the attention," he admits. His feet make their way over to me and he stares into my eyes intently. "But only because it's from you."

The confession isn't all that surprising, but it rocks me, nonetheless. Needing a bit of space to try and make sense of what I'm feeling, I step back and nod at the tent. "Thanks for setting that up." Looking around and spying some fallen branches, I grab a few and show them to Carter. "I'll get some firewood."

Carter's peaceful expression shutters slightly, but he nods and lets me move around him. "That would be great. I'll get everything else ready."

"Okay," I breathe out. I spend the next fifteen minutes gathering what I hope will be useful firewood, trying to make sense of the emotions swirling around inside me. Carter is amazing, and he deserves the type of person who will recognize that. I do, and he has mentioned many times that he thinks highly of me, but what if I decide three months from now that I'm done with small towns and miss life in the city? I haven't felt even a twinge of envy when I've seen posts from my so-called friends on social media about parties and other events, but maybe that will change in time. Hurting Carter by starting something with him and then bailing isn't something I can do, and as much as I enjoy what we're exploring together, it's not fair to either of us if we catch feelings and then I end it.

When I make my way back to the clearing, Carter has everything set up, including having dragged a fallen log over to where we'll set up the fire. I'm a little sad I missed that particular display of manliness, but my walk in the woods was more important. "I got wood," I announce, trying not to snicker like a twelve-year-old boy at my choice of words.

Carter is less able to hide his amusement, but takes the bundle from my arms without commenting on it. "Thank you."

After arranging the wood and getting the kindling ready, he lights the fire and I watch in amazement as it catches fairly quickly. "Wow," I exclaim, taking a seat on the log. The flames climb rapidly and glow from blue to orange, the warmth emanating from them staving off the chill that had started to creep in now that the sun has disappeared behind the mountains. "You're really good at this camping thing, huh?"

Carter smiles wistfully as he sits next to me. "I do all right." His expression turns a bit sorrowful as he stares into the fire. "My dad took me out a lot. Just like with woodworking, he taught me everything I know about camping."

Bumping his knee with mine, I smile over at him. "Tell me more about it."

Carter's face lights up at my request, the glow from his face rivaling that of the fire. "Yeah?" At my nod, he settles into the log and turns to me. "Dad always loved camping, even in his home country he would camp when it was freezing out. Mom wouldn't let him take me out for overnights in the snow until I was older, but once he did I could see why he loved it. When it's warmer, the forest is alive with so many different animals and sounds, but in the winter, there's a peacefulness that settles over it, over you." He looks at me bashfully. "Probably sounds a bit silly."

"No," I tell him honestly. As much as I love my parents, their letting me do my own thing sometimes had me longing for more of their company, something Carter seems to have gotten in abundance from his father. "It sounds really nice, and very different from the kind of environments I spent way too much time in. You definitely don't feel a sense of peace when you're out at a club."

Carter looks at me, his brow furrowed in thought. "What do you feel?"

Shrugging a shoulder, I try to think of an analogy for it. My body starts to sway involuntarily as I describe the atmosphere of a dance club. "Probably a lot like what the forest in summer is like. Alive, thriving. The beat pulses through your body and you can't help but move along with it."

Carter shakes his head and points at my chest. "No, what do *you* feel when you're at a club?"

Thinking back on all the times I've spent out on the town, I can't remember feeling the same sense of life that I just described to him, not for a while anyway. "I used to feel that energy and electricity in the air, and from time to time I still do." Swallowing thickly, I think about what emotion I felt most over the last few years when I would go out on the town. "More than that though, I think I was lonely. Like I could be in a club or bar, surrounded by people, noise, and flashing lights, and all the while I felt totally and completely alone." Blinking away the bit of moisture in my eyes, I turn to Carter to see his gaze fixed on me. "Does that sound absurd?" It does to me, but as I watch Carter shake his head emphatically, I can see he doesn't agree.

"No," he confesses. He reaches over and pulls me closer, tucking me into his side. "It sounds familiar."

Looking up at him, I offer a sad smile. "Fun trip this is turning out to be. I thought we came out here to clear my head, not sink the two of us into depression."

Carter huffs a laugh and rolls his eyes. "I'll tell you what my sister always tells me. You need to feel your feelings, even the messy ones." He continues to hold me close and smiles at me. "And I'm not depressed. How could I be when I'm with you?"

At that declaration, I can't possibly not kiss him. As I lean up, my lips slide against his, and the sadness from earlier is forgotten as I lose myself in the feel of him. The kiss is far less hungry than ones we've experienced before, but it is no less intense. Instead of it being fueled by lust, although there is a healthy amount of that, there is also an underlying sense that this is a lot more than just something we're doing to bolster his confidence. When his hands move to cup my face, I feel almost precious, like I'm something to be cherished, or beloved. No one besides my parents has ever made me feel this way, and even then it was always tempered by the idea that I was disappointing them somehow with my behavior and choices. Once again the thought of disappointing the man in front of me creeps into my mind, sending a sharp stab into my heart. The feeling is so unpleasant that I pull back, not wanting to conflate that feeling with kissing Carter.

I duck my head to try and hide my pain, but Carter sees it just like he seems to see just about everything about me. "What happened? You were here and then … you were somewhere else." He cups my cheek again and pulls my eyes to his. "Talk to me, *Elskling.*"

Hearing the foreign word roll so sweetly off his

tongue makes me feel a little better, but admitting the truth will be hard, especially since it means having to face worries I shouldn't be having. I'm feeling a lot of things for Carter, and none of them are casual, so knowing that I will probably disappoint him eventually like I do everyone else has my stomach feeling sour. "I just…" The words get stuck in my throat as I look at him. He's so kind, caring, and selfless, and here he is again looking after me when I'm supposed to be helping him out, not the other way around. "You've been so great, letting me stay with you and helping me try to figure out my life. I don't want to disappoint you."

Carter looks taken aback by my confession. "How on Earth do you think you could ever disappoint me? You've brought more fun into my life in the last month than I ever thought possible." I wince at his confession because while I like being fun, that was all I was good for in the past. Not much has changed it seems. "More than that, though," he says, giving me a look that tells me he knows exactly what I was thinking, "you've shown me that I can feel good about the person I am and that I deserve to go after what I want." He grips my chin in his hand and stares me down. "You do, too, you know. You deserve everything."

Nodding, I try to put the bad feelings back in a box, but can't quite manage to do so. "For right now, can you just hold me?"

Carter smiles and holds me tightly once again. "Nothing would make me happier." As I stare across the flames, sinking into the comfort provided by the man next to me, I can't help but feel that he's telling me the truth. And sitting here next to each other in front of the fire, just like him, I'm not sure anything could ever make me happier.

Chapter Seventeen

Carter

Holding Billie while we sat in front of the fire last night was like a dream come true. Ever since the moment we went out on a hike a few weeks back, I have literally had dreams about taking her camping, and showing her one of my favorite things to do while also providing her with an opportunity to clear her head a bit was just as amazing as I knew it would be. After she confessed her fear that she might disappoint me, there was no way I was going to let that fly. Telling her how wonderful she is and how she deserves the world felt as natural as holding her in my arms did, and I was very close to confessing just how much I care for her. But it wasn't the right time. After having lost my parents, I know that there is never really a wrong time to tell someone just how much you care about them, but somehow telling Billie that I'm falling in love with her while she was experiencing a moment of existential crisis didn't feel right. It felt selfish, and I can hold myself back if it means doing what's best for her.

Instead of confessing my feelings, I continued to keep her close, fed her a nice dinner of campfire steak and potatoes, and tucked us both in for sleep. Sharing a tent with Billie and not turning it into more was difficult, but she seemed legitimately tired and after a more subdued kiss goodnight, she fell asleep surprisingly fast. For as much as she complained about not having her eye mask, silk pillowcase, and everything else she needs to get her eight hours, she seemed to drift off peacefully enough. It took me much longer, and no matter how hard I tried to clear my mind and concentrate on nothing but her even breathing, all I could think about was how I wanted to wrap my arms around her and keep them there all night long. Eventually, I fell into a decent sleep, stirring only occasionally at the intermittent hooting of an owl and other nocturnal animal noises.

The sounds of the night forest have been replaced by louder ones from the early morning outdoors, and a jaw cracking yawn escapes me as my consciousness starts to come back online. As I stir, I feel a warm, heavy presence on top of me. Smiling, I gaze down at Billie who must have rolled half over me in the middle of the night. I'm certainly not complaining though as she shifts in her sleep and her body rubs up against mine, I can't help but react the way I always do when she's near. Despite being on top of my thickening cock, the woman sleeping next to me still slumbers peacefully. We lay like that for a while, me gritting my teeth with every shift of her body and every breathy moan as to not wake her with sounds of my own, but as the sun rises higher over the horizon and continues to light up the tent, she slowly blinks her eyes open.

"Good morning," she smiles. Her voice is raspy with sleep, her hair is matted in different directions, and she has a large crease on her cheek from where it lay against part of the blanket, but she's never looked more beautiful.

Returning her smile, I brush some hair out of her eyes with one hand while rubbing her back with another. "Good morning."

Her body shifts slightly and I stifle another groan as I get even harder. From the widening of her eyes and the fire I see igniting within them, Billie knows exactly which part of me is pushing against her thigh. A knowing smile spreads across her face as she peers down at me. "A very good morning, indeed," she says. Moving her hand so that it's running up and down the side of my torso, a sly smile plays on her face.

The tent and blankets I brought were warm enough for me to sleep just in a pair of sweats and a t-shirt, but even then the top was a little much and I ditched it halfway through the night. Feeling her warm hand smooth up and down my bare skin has me shivering and my internal body temperature ratcheting up with each pass. "Billie." Instead of her name coming out as a censure like I meant it to, my voice sounds low and feathery, like I'm two seconds away from begging her to keep going. When it comes to her, I wouldn't put it past me to do just that.

Billie moves again, flinging the blanket off the two of us and sliding her body away from mine just enough to be able to snake her hand lower and dip her fingers just inside the waistband of my sweats. "You want me to keep going?" She looks down at the tent in my sweats that grows higher by the second. "Because it sure looks like it."

All my blood is rushing south, and while I would like to stop her, tell her how I feel and that I want this to mean more than practice to her too, I can't really think of anything other than how good things feel between us. Being with her means something to me, and maybe that's enough for now. Her fingers swirl a little lower, and I can no longer think, only feel. "Please," I whisper.

Billie smirks, but there's a lot more than the usual sass in her eyes. There's affection too, and even though she might not be as far along with her feelings as I am, I'm confident that she'll get there eventually. "So polite," she remarks, her hand moving south and gripping me firmly. As her hand twists and tugs, working me into an even greater frenzy, a loud moan escapes my mouth and I pray that no hikers come by anytime soon. "Love to hear you moan, Viking." She leans down and takes my mouth in a punishing kiss. "Do you think I can make you scream? I'm very tempted to try."

Billie trails kisses down my chest, flicking her tongue over my nipple before continuing her journey south. She tugs my sweats lower, pulling my dick out from its cotton prison. Looking up at me for a moment, she winks before wrapping her hand around the base and licking a stripe up the underside of my cock. My head drops back against the hard ground, but I don't notice the thudding sound it makes. I'm too caught up in the flurry of sensations pulsing through my body. "God, that feels amazing."

My hand reaches down to cradle her head as she continues to work me with her tongue, slipping it through the slit at the top while she pumps me with her hand. My only experience with blowjobs is the one my ex from years ago attempted, abandoning it after a couple of licks and declaring that they "weren't for her." Billie is obviously not in the same camp because she seems to be enjoying it as much as I am. She hums contentedly as she nuzzles my hip and inhales the smell of me. Then she leans up and sucks on the tip before finally engulfing as much of me as she can into her warm mouth. As I slide inside and over her tongue, I can feel the base of my spine starting to tingle and rub her cheek to get her attention.

"Not gonna last much longer." She doesn't move off me and instead doubles down on her efforts, causing me to spill into her mouth as my vision whites out and I come with a shout. As I come back down from what has to be the best orgasm of my life, my eyes finally blink open to see Billie wiping the corner of her mouth with her finger before licking it clean. *Damn, that's hot.*

When she smirks, I realize I said that out loud, but I'm too blissed out to care. "Glad you approve" She smirks as she tucks my slightly softened cock back into my pants. Glancing up at her, I take in the flush of her skin and the heat in her gaze.

After a long inhale to catch my breath, I roll us so that her body is pinned under mine. "I more than approve." Pressing my lips to hers, I push my thigh between her legs and press down, swallowing her whimpers as I continue to work my mouth over hers. "In fact, I want to return the favor."

Billie raises her hips up to my leg, seeking her own pleasure. "It won't take much," she breathes out. "Having you in my mouth got me pretty close." Smiling, I shift my leg higher, earning a moan from Billie. Hearing her has me rock hard again already, and I rearrange myself so that it's my cock pressing into her center instead of my thigh. "Oh, yes, please."

Billie reaches down and whips the flimsy tank top she was wearing over her head and tosses it to the side. With so much beautiful olive skin on display, it's hard to know where to look first, but of course my eyes fall to her perfect breasts, saliva pooling at the thought of getting them into my mouth. Not wanting to deny myself or her any longer, I lean down and do just that. As I continue to lavish attention on one and then the other, teasing each dark red peak of her nipples with my tongue, my thrusts increase in speed and pressure. After another minute of performing that act, Billie tenses underneath me before shattering, crying my name out in a way that will be permanently seared into my brain. Nothing looks or sounds as beautiful as she does when she has an orgasm, and I can't wait to see the same expression and hear the same sounds over and over again as soon as possible.

Smiling down at her as she comes back to herself, I kiss her gently before rolling to the side and gathering her in my arms. When she's finally caught her breath, she looks up at me before lightly kissing my cheek. "Thank you," she tells me. She ducks her head against my chest and holds me almost as tightly as I do her. "Best wake-up ever."

"Absolutely," I agree. And if it were up to only me, we would wake up this way every day for the rest of our lives.

****

After the fun I had with Billie in the tent this morning, a smile has taken up permanent residence on my face. It was there as we drove back into town, as we went grocery shopping together, and especially as we had another round of getting each other off in my bedroom that afternoon. Even now as we make the trek up the driveway to my childhood home for dinner with Maya's family, the uneasiness I usually feel when visiting can't keep me from grinning like a sap.

Just as I'm about to knock, Billie elbows me in the side. When I look over at her, she gives me a pointed look. "You better wipe that smile off your face. You look like the cat that caught the canary," she admonishes.

"I can't help it," I confess with a shoulder shrug. "I'm an easily readable person and it's hard to hide how happy I am."

Billie blushes slightly, her eyes glazed with her own happiness, but she soon shakes it away. "I'm happy you're happy, but I don't feel like talking about what we're doing with Jake and Maya, and if you walk around with that shit-eating grin on your face, they'll definitely know something is going on."

"Fine," I breathe out. Making a huge show of wiping a hand down my face, I put on a mock sad face. "Do I look like my normal self now?"

A chuckle escapes from her lips and she knocks

on the door. "You're such a dork." She rolls her eyes, but can't hide the fact that she's smiling from me.

That I can make this beautiful woman smile has me feeling ten feet tall and capable of toppling trees with my bare hands. The bright smile she wanted me to hide so badly comes out in full force again just as my sister opens the door to greet us. Her sky blue eyes ping between Billie and me for a moment before she smiles slyly. "You two look pretty pleased about something," she announces, stepping to the side and ushering us into the house.

Billie nods and walks inside, dropping her purse on the entry table. "We are. They had a two for one deal on kettle corn at the market. It's our favorite thing to snack on while we watch trashy television." It isn't a lie, but it feels wrong not to be able to declare how I feel about Billie and what I suspect that she might be starting to feel for me, like my skin is too tight all of a sudden. Of course, I haven't even confessed it to the woman herself yet, so maybe I'm getting bent out of shape over nothing.

Maya shakes her head as the three of us walk into the living room where JJ and Jake are on the floor playing with magnetic tiles. Taking a look around the updated room normally has me feeling a little unsteady, but as I take in the old mantle that my father carved offset by the bookcases I put in myself, I can't help but feel like everything is as it should be. The old and new together, creating a happy atmosphere for my sister and her family. When I look over at Maya, the look of contentment on her face helps solidify the feeling. Soon her expression morphs into one of annoyance and she pokes my arm. "I still can't believe you watch that stuff with Billie when you wouldn't watch *The Bachelor* with me."

"Her commentary is funnier," I confess, my shoulder bobbing lightly. It is, but the real reason I like watching it is because it allows me to spend more time with Billie. From the look Maya shoots me, she's not really buying my commentary excuse either. Luckily, JJ runs up to me and hugs my legs before she gets a chance to say anything more about it, though I know she will eventually.

As it turns out, eventually comes right after our shared meal when I offer to do the dishes. Dinner conversation mostly revolved around Maya and Jake's wedding happening in a few months, and even though it is going to be a small affair taking place in the town square, there were a lot of details that Maya wanted to discuss with us. Well, mostly Billie to get her opinion, but occasionally she would ask for mine as well. JJ had been bored through most of the meal, so it wasn't surprising that he finished his food in record time, eventually climbing out of his booster seat and going over to Billie to ask her to play with him in his room. Of course, she immediately agreed, looking so excited that he was warming up to her that I didn't have the heart to intrude on their time, even though I've been missing hanging out with my nephew too. Jake accompanied her, and I assumed Maya did as well, but the minute I am elbow deep in soapy water, she appears from the dining room and pounces.

"So, you and Billie?" she asks again. When I hazard a glance in her direction, I see that her expression isn't accusatory, but there is definitely an edge to her voice that I hadn't expected. She's made hints about the two of us together before, but she always seemed happy about it in the past, so this new tone is surprising.

Suddenly the casserole dish is my highest priority, and I focus my attention on getting it as clean as possible. "What about us?" My stomach sinks as I realize that I'm a little worried about what my sister will have to say. I may be older, but between losing our parents and raising a kid mostly on her own, Maya had to mature a lot more quickly than other women her age, and she doesn't beat around the bush.

Maya sighs as she leans against the counter near the sink. "You know what I'm asking Carter," she scolds. Her mom voice is in full effect and it works like a charm. Guilt blooms in my chest, but over what I have no idea. "While I fully support the idea of the two of you having fun, I can tell that it's getting a lot more serious than that, at least for you." She pauses to lightly touch my shoulder. "I don't want to see you get hurt."

"I won't." My voice is insistent, but the conviction I hoped to feel isn't quite there. It might be if I had more evidence that the woman I'm in love with felt the same way about me, but I don't. *And you won't anytime soon if you don't talk to her.*

Maya sighs heavily. "Carter, you don't even know if she's staying in town. Would you be willing to do a long distance relationship? Or move if she wanted to be back in Denver?"

Both are scenarios I hadn't thought were even a remote possibility. Billie fit into my life so naturally that I hadn't even considered if I would fit into hers. From what she's told me, she wouldn't want to go back to clubbing and fancy parties, but maybe she just needed a break from it and will want that again eventually. Would she really want some wannabe lumberjack on her arm as she waltzed into a club looking like a million dollars? The possibility of that is remote at best. While I want to be with her more than anything, the idea that she would eventually tire of me and my more reclusive ways as me hesitating again. I can make furniture anywhere, but I love my family, the shop, and the small town I currently live in. Being with Billie in Denver would mean sacrificing all that, and that's if she even wanted me there with her to begin with.

Maya must sense me spiraling, because she shakes my shoulder and forces me to look at her. "I'm not saying that will happen, but maybe don't fall so hard until you know for sure what her plans are."

I nod and Maya leaves me to finish the dishes and stew in my uncertainty. As I do, I realize that what she's asked of me isn't possible. I can't prevent myself from falling hard for Billie because I already have.

Chapter Eighteen

Billie

Carter has been quieter than normal ever since the dinner we had at Jake and Maya's a few days ago. He's still the same caring, thoughtful individual, but he's been a little more withdrawn. He's also been spending a lot more time working in the workshop, so I've barely seen him over the last three evenings, and when I do he's so tired he gives me a peck on the lips before heading off to bed. For a moment, I thought that he might have regretted what we did while we were camping, but he was so happy that I can't believe that's it. I was happy too. How can you not be after a fantastic orgasm with someone you care about? Now, though, Carter's distance has me climbing the walls, but fortunately, I still have my wily ways about me and came up with a way to fix it. At least, I hope it will fix it.

While Carter has been occupied in his workshop with orders and whatever else he's been working on to avoid me, I've been busy making plans for the perfect date for the two of us, and by date I mean sex. Carter is so selfless and caring that I want to be that for him too, and while I could make us dinner or take us out to a fancy restaurant, I think this will be better. During the few hours that Maya has been at the shop so far this week, I've gone out shopping as both therapy and as a means to get things ready for the big night tonight. A few candles from the shop downstairs, a discreet purchase from the local pharmacy, and a trip to the local lingerie store means everything is ready to go. Now all I need is the man himself to come upstairs.

If left to his own devices, I am sure that Carter would spend another late night in his workshop, but I can't let that happen. Grabbing my phone from the bathroom counter, I fire off a text asking him to come home. No excuse will be needed because I know that if I ask something of him, he'll do it. Not in a blindly obedient way, but in an "I care about you and want you to be happy" way. Instead of examining the floaty feeling I get in my chest when I consider that, I give myself one last once over in the mirror.

My hair is down and curled into chunky waves, but I ditched any attempt to do make-up, knowing that I will be sweating it all off anyway. Or at least, I hope I will. With one final adjustment to the dark pink, mesh bustier, I stride over to the door to wait for my man. My feet stumble as the thought crosses my mind. *My man?* It sure feels an awful lot like Carter belongs to me, but maybe that's because I want to belong to him. This was supposed to just be an exercise in boosting his confidence, and maybe it still is for him, but it's definitely become a lot more than that to me.

Before I can ponder that any further, I hear footsteps on the landing and the knob jiggle as it starts to turn. Arranging myself as sexily as possibly while trying to not look like I'm trying too hard, I rest a hand on my hip while the other plays at the swell of my breasts, wanting his attention there even though the lingerie I am in puts just about everything on display.

When Carter strides in and sees me, his steps halt and his jaw literally drops open. His eyes move up and down my body like a caress that is causing me to shiver before he's even had a chance to touch me. As I continue to run my finger over the tops of my breasts and along my collarbone, I walk over to him, my bare feet padding on the hardwood. I thought about wearing heels, but that would be just one more thing to take off and I want to get down to business as soon as possible. He was so happy after we had sex the other day and I want him to be happy again, but more than that, I want to show him how much he's come to mean to me. I'm not ready to say it with words just yet, so this is what I have to use for now.

"What's this all about?" he asks. His voice is raspy, and one look down at the growing bulge in his jeans lets me know it's from lust, and when I gaze up into his eyes, the fire I see burning behind the forest green confirms it.

When I'm right in front of him, I push him against the door, closing it and flicking the lock. Nothing is going to interrupt us tonight. No nephews or surprise visits from family, no overtime at the job. Nothing. Sliding my hands up and down the thin material of his work tee, I stop and rub at his nipples for a moment before heading south to cup his bulge, pressing down on the hardness. When he hisses through his teeth and bucks into my hand, I know I've got him right where I want him, aching for me. "This is about you working too hard," I explain. My hand squeezes him through his jeans, eliciting another deeper groan from his throat. "I missed you." The confession is followed up with more stroking.

Carter's head has dropped back against the door and his eyes are closed, but he reaches over to me and cups my face, stroking the skin of my cheek with his thumb. When his eyes open again, I see a lot more than need and desire. I'm pretty sure I see love, and while it feels scary, it also feels so wonderful that I can't stop myself from continuing. Emotions can be examined later. Right now, I want to make him feel good. "I missed you too," he breathes out.

Drawing me closer to him, he lowers himself to me and plants a kiss on my lips. It's not slow and languid like I thought it might be after seeing all of that affection in his gaze. Instead it is hard and desperate, like he's not sure if he'll get more opportunities like this in the future. He will, he just doesn't know it yet. I want him to know it, want Carter to feel assured that I will always be here for him like he's been here for me ever since I arrived. He was there for me before that too. His smiling face on social media was the little bit of levity I needed when I was missing my friend and working a job I didn't love. But can I really give him that when I'm not sure what I'm doing yet? I may not be able to give him the words or a solid sense of the future, but I can give him this.

Pressing my hands against his chest, I break our kiss. My hands reach down and start to undo the buckle of his belt, the clinking sound and our ragged breaths the only things that can be heard in the apartment. As I slowly unzip his pants, I arch a brow at him. "Tell me you don't want this, and I'll stop."

Carter's head moves side to side slowly, his mouth quirking to one side. "I don't think I've wanted anything more in my entire life." The words weaken my knees, but I manage to stay standing as I reach into his pants and grab ahold of him. I knew he went commando, but having such easy access to him is still just as thrilling as if it had been a pleasant surprise. My hand continues to stroke him as his hands begin to explore my breasts. His thumbs tease at my nipples while my hand works him harder. Squeezing my legs together to relieve the pressure, I reach my free hand up and drag his mouth back to mine. Our lips collide seconds before his tongue darts out and I suck it into my mouth.

I work his tongue like I work his cock, faster and harder until he's so stiff and swollen in my hand that I know he's going to come any second. "Okay, Viking," I whisper in his ear. "Come for me."

With a grunt, Carter spills over my hand, a little

getting on his pants, but from the look of absolute euphoria on his face, he doesn't care at all. I bring my hand to my lips to taste him, loving the salty sweet flavor as it travels over my tongue. Carter watches me, his eyes darkening as I lick one finger clean and then the other. "God, you are amazing," He reaches up and grabs the back of his shirt, swiftly pulling it off and using it to wipe the rest of my hand clean.

"I wasn't done you know," I remark as he tosses his soiled shirt to the side. He steps out of his jeans and shoes before kicking those away as well.

When he steps towards me, a smirk plays at his mouth. "Don't worry. Plenty more where that came from." Carter winks and leans down to scoop me up into his arms before striding over to his bedroom.

My head dips back and I chuckle at him. "That's the kind of attitude I like to see, Viking." Carter tosses me onto my bed, and I get my first full look of him completely naked. He is hard muscle and soft skin, and I love every inch of him. He comes to the bed and prowls over me, leaning down to kiss me briefly before he moves south. His kisses move over my chest and then he pulls one of my nipples into his mouth, mesh material and all, before working to the other side. He unbuttons my corset and tosses it away, leaning back down and dipping his head, moving from one breast to the other for what feels like forever until I am writhing beneath him. "Please," I beg.

Carter chuckles, the warm air from his mouth skating over my wet nipple, making another part of me even wetter than it was before. "I'll always give you what you ask for, *Elskling*." After he said the word again the other day, I looked up the translation. It means *darling*, and when I'm with him, that's what I feel like.

Cater kisses my belly lightly before hooking his

thumbs into the straps of my thong and tugging. Lifting my hips to help him, I smile excitedly as he tosses them over his shoulder. Whatever caused this newfound confidence, I like the look of it. Or maybe I just like the look of him. Either way, I'm happy to see him realizing what an amazing person he is. My thoughts about him are disrupted slightly as he starts to skim his hands over the tops of my thighs, dipping his fingers around to cup my ass a little before he spreads my legs out and settles his shoulders between them.

He licks his lips, but hesitates. Glancing up at me, he looks sheepish for the first time all night. "I'm not sure exactly what I'm doing, but I'm going to do my best."

"Have at it." I wave a hand at my now bare pussy. "We here at The Billie Kochev Institute of Sexual Education are all about giving you as many opportunities as you need to learn your craft."

Carter laughs, the air whooshing from his lungs and over my clit causing it to pulse. "Good to know."

After that, any laughter between us dies as he slowly drags his tongue from my hole up to my small bundle of nerves, giving it extra special attention. For someone who has little experience, he's a natural at eating me out, doing more of something when I moan with pleasure or less of something when I give a less than stellar response. He's so attentive that that alone has me getting closer to climaxing, only I want to do it with him inside me.

Reaching over to his nightstand, I dip a hand inside and grab one of the few boxes of condoms I purchased yesterday. Cupping his cheek, I pull his gaze up to mine as he's mid lick, loving the feel of his skin against my hand. "Want you inside me now."

He nods shakily, but after tossing the box of condoms to him, his expression goes from hesitation to confusion. "I know for a fact I didn't have these in my nightstand." Still, he grabs a condom, tears the foil and slides one on expertly.

"I wanted to be prepared, so I bought some and put them in every room in the apartment. I had no idea where we would end up having sex, so I wanted to be ready for any eventuality."

Carter smiles wickedly as he lines himself up to my center. "You know what that means," he says, sliding in an inch. "We have to do it wherever we find a box."

Nodding as he glides in further, the stretch feeling so good that I groan audibly, I grab his neck and bring his forehead down to mine. "Sounds like a plan."

Carter pushes the rest of the way in, grunting when he finally bottoms out. "You feel so good," he breathes out. Slowly, he drags his cock back out, inch by glorious inch, before slamming it back in again. I lean up and kiss him, loving the taste of cinnamon that always seems to be there, like it's inherent to him. Carter's tongue drives into my mouth as his cock drives into my body. He started slow, but some of the desperation from earlier is back and he's pounding away at me like a man possessed. It feels amazing, and I never want him to stop.

"So good," I agree, my hips meeting him thrust for thrust. My hands rake down his back so that I can cup his ass, helping him push into me even harder than before. I can feel my muscles start to tighten, the telltale sign that my release is near. As if he can sense it, he grabs one of my legs, throwing it over his shoulder so that he can get even deeper without me having to say a thing. After two more pumps of his hips, every muscle in my body coils tightly before springing loose in the most wonderful feeling of ecstasy. Lightning strikes appear behind my eyelids and I shout his name, but he doesn't stop. Carter keeps going until he's wrung at least two more orgasms from me, finally going over the precipice himself and spilling into the condom as he kisses me on the lips.

After what could be seconds or hours, my mind finally comes back online in time to see Carter tying off the condom and tossing it in the wastebasket near the bed. He rolls over and pulls my back against his chest, draping his arm over me and humming contentedly. "Will you stay with me?"

My throat is thick with unspoken needs, like the need for him to mean more than just tonight. "Uh huh," I manage to get out. Settling into the cradle of his arms, I try to relax and enjoy the moment, not knowing whether or not I will get many more like it again.

Chapter Nineteen

Carter

Early morning light peeking through the blinds of my bedroom window and the sound of increased traffic noise outside stir me from the deepest, most peaceful sleep I have ever had. Shifting slightly, I momentarily startle and panic when I hear a grumble of discontent come from just below my head, only to remember that Billie is in bed with me and what we shared last night wasn't a dream. My eyes peek open and as I spy the mass of tangled brown waves cascading over her face and onto my chest, I smile to myself, not quite believing my good luck at having such an amazing woman clinging to me. Gingerly, I lift my hand and move the hair off her face. The action causes her to stir a bit, and my smile pulls wider when I see the look of serenity on her face as she burrows closer to me and settles back into sleep.

For long moments, I watch her in slumber. Over her nose, there are a few faint freckles that you wouldn't be able to see unless you were this close to her, and I thank my lucky stars that I am and have the opportunity to catalog her features. The apples of her cheeks are a natural, rosy pink and her upper lip is shaped in the most perfect Cupid's bow I have ever seen. My eyes move upward and see a few tiny wisps of hair at the top of her hairline, and something about the thin, barely-there strands reminds me that even though this woman is strong, smart, and sexy, she is also sweet and can make herself vulnerable just as she did last night. Billie's confidence in the bedroom could make someone think she wasn't vulnerable at all, but there were moments when we were together last night, like when she would say 'please' or look into my eyes as I entered her when I could see that her walls were down. It made the whole experience that much better, and I can't wait to repeat it.

My fingers twitch with the need to touch her, so I do. Lightly, I brush my fingers over the smooth skin of her arms, relishing the sight of the goosebumps that break out over her skin. When my eyes flick back up to her face, I watch her long, dark lashes flutter for a few seconds before her eyes blink open and stare up into mine. Her mouth turns up at the corners as she wakes a little more. "Good morning," she says, her voice rough with sleep.

There are so many words on the tip of my tongue, words about how I have fallen in love with her, how I wished for someone special a long time ago and that I now know that it's her, but I'm not quite ready to put a voice to them just as I'm sure she's not ready to hear them yet. Billie's confidence extends to a lot of things, but I get the feeling she may not be completely aware of just how deserving she is of love. Instead of telling her everything that is written on my heart, I say words that are true in this moment. "I need you, *Elskling.*"

Billie's eyes widen and sparkle for a moment, emotions passing over her face I can't quite decipher but wish to God I could because I want to know everything that goes on in this woman's mind and every wish that she holds in her heart. She continues to stare at me a moment before her expression shifts to one that's more mischievous than awestruck. "Do you now?" she asks, her palm sliding down my torso until she's gripping the hard wood of my erection that's been there since the moment I woke up and felt her in my arms and starts to pump her fist.

My hips buck into her hand as I reach up and cup her face. Gazing into her cocoa eyes, I make my tone as serious as possible so she can hear the truth in my words.

"Always."

Before she can say anything to dispute me, I lean down and seal my lips over hers. Billie's hand stutters for a moment as she gets lost in our kiss and I couldn't care less. When I said I needed her, I meant it to be about more than sex. Sex with her is amazing and something I know will only get better and more amazing as time passes, but I also need her in my life in other ways. Her smile brightens my day no matter how long or hard it has been and her presence eases the ache of my loneliness, not just because she is another person in the room, but because she is the *best* possible person that could ever be in the room with me. Her care and attention make the grief I still sometimes carry with me that much lighter because she makes everything lighter. Every burden is lessened because of who she is and I need her in my life more than I need anything else in this world.

The realization of that has my lips faltering slightly as we kiss, and Billie takes the short break as an opportunity to move things along. Pushing the sheets back, she swings one leg over me until she's straddling my torso and running my dick through her wet folds. With a loud groan, I grip onto her hips and push my growing feelings beneath the surface, focusing instead on making this experience as good for her as I possibly can. Just her moving on top of me like this already has my mind blowing wide with new sensations, but she might need more than that. When I look up at her face as it hovers above mine, the sultry expression she wears makes me wonder if my previous thought was actually correct. Each time she grinds down on me, I see her pupils dilate that much wider and her breath is coming in short and fast. "I'm getting close already," she breathes out.

Her hand reaches between us and she moves me

until my tip is hitting her clit in a way that makes her face light up and a low moan skate across her lips. "Hell, yes," I mutter. "Use me to get yourself off." It's hotter than anything I have ever seen or experienced, and if she wants to use me as her own personal sex toy, I am all for that.

Billie doesn't say anything but nods, her movements picking up speed until finally she opens her mouth in a silent scream, her eyes boring into mine as she comes, looking like a goddess that I don't deserve but will do everything in my power to keep. As she comes down, she lightly brushes her lips against mine and shifts over me, but I still her with my hands that are still on her hips and start her moving again. As she slides, the tip of my dick accidently slips into her and even though it feels amazing, I pull back and start to reach over to the nightstand for protection. "Wait," she commands, her hand on my arm. When I look back at her, she bites her lower lip in thought before leaning down to whisper in my ear. "I'm clean and on the pill. We can ditch the condoms if you want."

Drawing my hand back and placing it on her lower back, I stare into her face and try to read her expression. It's nearly inscrutable, but I definitely don't see any doubt. "I'm good with that." *More than good.* "But are you sure? I'm clean too," I mention for good measure. With as little experience as I have it would be a wonder if I weren't, but just because I haven't been with a lot of people doesn't mean I'm not still overly cautious Carter.

Billie smiles and nods before slipping up my still hard dick and impaling herself on it in one swift move. The first feel of her warm center against my sensitive skin could be described as silk if the light, slick material had an iron grip, one that has me needing to do a mental inventory of my workshop to prevent myself from going off immediately. When she starts to move, the need to come increases and my eyes nearly roll back in my head from all the pleasure I'm experiencing. "God, this feels..." I don't have words for how it feels because my mind is scrambled from all the amazing sensations rolling through my body.

Billie leans down and rests her forehead against mine as she continues to swivel her hips. "It does," she agrees. Her lips brush against mine as she reaches back and starts to play with my heavy sac. The addition of her hand on me has the tension in my body rising and I can't stop myself from thrusting up into her. The move makes her whimper against my mouth. "Yes, more of that, please."

My hands smooth up her back and around to her breasts where I tease at her nipples with my fingers, thrusting in to her again and again until we're both covered in a sheen of sweat from the exertion. The muscles of my body start to tighten in preparation for my orgasm, "Close," I mutter. In an effort to get her off first, I lean up and pull one breast into my mouth while I pinch her other nipple, my free hand sliding between us to thumb at her clit. It doesn't take more than a few flicks before she shatters. The sight of her getting off paired with a satisfied moan leaving her lips has me tipping over the edge and coming with her, spilling into her with a grunt as she continues to bounce up and down on my dick until she's milked me dry.

When we've both come down and caught our breath, Billie rolls to the side and lays next to me. The loss of her body heat and the sweat evaporating from my skin causes me to shiver. My head turns to Billie and her face lights up with something before she moves off the bed. "Wait right here," she tells me. As I watch her gloriously naked body retreat from my room, I sit up and wonder where she thinks I would possibly go when I have someone like her in bed with me. A minute later, she comes back carrying a large box with a red ribbon over it and places it on my lap. "I got this for you. I was going to give it to you last night, but we, uh, got a little caught up."

Her cheeks flush a deeper pink than they already were and I stifle a smile at her getting a little shy talking about us having sex while we're both sitting in my bed without a stitch of clothing on. "You didn't have to get me anything," I tell her.

Her shoulder bobs and she scoots closer to me. "I wanted to," she confesses. She taps the lid of the box and looks at me expectantly and if I'm not mistaken, with a bit of nerves as well. "Now open it."

Nodding, I pull off the ribbon and lift the lid of the box, my eyes widening when I see what's inside. "My dad's flannels?" But when I pull the familiar material out of the box, it isn't a series of shirts that come out but is instead a large quilt. As my eyes roam over the blanket, I see each large square is made of a different shirt that had been owned by my father and worn by me. The back is reinforced with a thick, dark green material that feels soft against my skin, but it's the front that I can't stop looking at. Lifting the blanket to my nose, I inhale and even though I am sure it's only in my mind, I swear I can still smell the woodsy scent that clung to my dad wherever he went still lingering there. My throat gets thick with emotion and moisture gathers in my eyes, not just at the bittersweet memory of my dad, but at the thoughtfulness of the woman next to me.

"Do you hate it?" she asks, her voice small and quiet.

Her voice should only ever be bright and happy,

just like her, and especially when I'm getting choked up because of how incredible the gift she got me is. "No I love it. I love…" The words trail off because I want to tell her I love her, but this moment seems too beautiful to shatter with that confession. This is about her thoughtfulness and care, not about my feelings. "Thank you, Billie." Pushing the box aside, I pull her next to me and spread the blanket over the both of us. "This is incredible and easily the best gift anyone has ever given me. My dad would love it, and both my parents would have loved you."

Billie's eyes dance with happiness at the declaration and she smiles. Her expression turns playful before she swipes her hand dramatically across her forehead and I hear a breath whoosh out of her lungs. "Thank goodness. I was worried that you might be upset that I had your dad's shirts cut up."

Shaking my head, I lean down and kiss her lips gently. She's trying to lighten the mood, but my feelings are too serious for me to take the bait. "No, *Elskling*. You've given me a way to keep my dad close, and not just with this." She has shown me a way to honor my dad in my own way and in my own style while also making sure I would be able to have the safety and comfort that the old way provided. "You've given me a lot, and I hope you know how much I appreciate it."

"I do.". The seriousness on her face tells me she means it, but her mouth soon pulls into a smirk before she snuggles closer to me under the blanket. With a wink, she reaches down and squeezes my thigh with her hand before trailing it up my leg. "Maybe after a little rest you can *show* me how much you appreciate it."

Returning her smile, I take her lips in a kiss. "Why wait?" As we slip down into the bed and I pull the blanket over our heads, I proceed to show her just how grateful I am for her gift, and for her.

Chapter Twenty

Billie

The first night Carter and I slept together was amazing, so amazing in fact that in the month since then, we haven't spent a single night apart from one another. Whether it's in his bed or mine, we end the day with sex and snuggles before we both slip into the sweetest slumber either of us have ever had. At least, it's been the sweetest for me. From the contented look on Carter's face when we wake up every morning, it's safe to assume he feels the same way. He is my new favorite body pillow, and I'm already used to his presence not only in my bed, but also in my heart. The desire to spill my feelings is hard to resist, but I do it every day because even though I'm pretty sure I'm in love with Carter, I still have no idea of what I'm supposed to do with my life.

The party planning didn't pan out, and since then no other ideas have really come to me. I enjoy working at Hodgepodge. Each day brings a new set of people to chat with and steer around the store, helping them find exactly what they need or didn't know they wanted until I showed it to them. It also allows me to explore my more creative side by talking with the artisans and always keeping an eye out for new and exciting items that the store might want to showcase. As much as I love my time there, it's not exactly what I went to school for and if my parents weren't already disappointed in me for getting so off track in life, they certainly would be if I wasted the education they paid for. *Maybe they would just be happy that you're happy.*

The thought springs to mind just as Maya returns from her lunch break, a bag from the local craft supply store dangling from one hand. No doubt it's full of more yarn for her to create baby booties and stuffed animals with for her crochet business. Ever since the beginning of August when JJ started going to preschool and I've gotten the hang of things at the shop, she's been spending more of her time on her own thing and doing quite well if the sheer number of orders she's been fulfilling are any indication. As she bounces over to the front counter, a grin comes over her face when she sees me. "Hello," she says cheerily. Her smile is so bright it almost hurts to look at it, but it's impossible not to return it either.

"Welcome back," I tell her. Grabbing the bag, I peek inside and chuckle at the multiple skeins of yarn that confirm my earlier suspicions. "I can see that your lunch break was productive."

Maya laughs and starts to unpack her purchase. "Very." Brown, black, and white yarn is pulled out along with other smaller items that she will use to make something spectacular that I have no name for. "I'm starting on two pairs of brown bear booties with matching stuffies today for a couple who is expecting twins. How cute will that be?"

"So cute," I agree. Picking up the brown, I run my hand over the soft fabric and smile at the thought of asking Maya to make booties for my own baby someday. When I picture my future child, they have moss green eyes just like their dad's, but that won't become a reality if I don't get my act together. When my eyes move up to hers, she smiles knowingly at me but says nothing. I'm not sure what her brother has told her about us, but it's clear that she knows *something* is going on. Still, I'm glad she's not commenting on it. Unlike the yarn that is meticulously wrapped and orderly, my thoughts and feelings are a tangled mess. Maya's expression is the exact opposite, full of confidence and a certainty of self I can only imagine having. "You look happy."

The emotion is practically radiating from her every pore as her smile grows. "I am happy," she states matter-of-factly. Her eyes study mine for a moment before she speaks again. "Are you?"

The question has me immediately thinking about Carter and my mouth pulls at the sides. Spending time with him makes me happy, working here with him at the store makes me happy, but when I start to think about my professional future, the question draws a blank and makes me feel a little less sure about everything else in my life. My shoulder lifts as I struggle to answer the question. "I don't know. Maybe?" The words sound so stupid when I say them aloud. I am beyond privileged to be in the position I am, spending time with an amazing guy while working a job that is satisfying and living in a great town. Anyone else would probably answer with a resounding *Yes,* but I can't get past my own jumbled thoughts to say it.

Maya comes around the counter and pulls me into a hug. She smells like apple pie and my stomach growls at the thought of having a slice. She chuckles at the sound and pulls back, but not before giving me a pointed look. "Well, you either are or you are really spectacular at faking it, but I don't think you're that good of an actress. No offense."

"None taken," I admit. My heart feels happy, but my mind is another story, so the answer to her question is still a bit of an unknown.

I look over at Maya to see her eyes narrowing at me slightly. "Have I thanked you for your help at the shop? I know you had a rough couple of days in the beginning, but you have been invaluable. In fact, the only person I've seen run things as well as you have is my mom." Maya's eyes get a little glassy, but she blinks away the tears that threaten. "They would have loved you, you know? My parents."

"Carter said the same thing," I confess. The amount of happiness that brought me is immeasurable. That he thinks his parents would not only approve, but love me, makes me feel a sense of belonging that I've been missing outside of my own family.

She nods like this isn't news to her and simply smiles at me. "Well, he's a pretty smart guy, and for whatever it's worth, I've never seen him happier than I have since you showed up."

My heart soars at her words, but I'm not sure what to say in return, so I stand there and nod dumbly. All of this information is helping to clear away the mess in my head, but not entirely. The back door opens and at the sound of heavy footsteps, we both turn to see Carter striding in carrying a toy box. My heart nearly beats out of my chest with excitement at seeing him, but the thought that he deserves more than a woman with a giant question mark where her future is concerned creeps in and dampens it slightly.

As he strides closer, I can see the color of his eyes is slightly more jade than evergreen today, and I wonder if it isn't the happiness Maya mentioned broadcasting out through them. "Good afternoon, ladies," he says. He nods at his sister before leaning down and kissing my temple. We haven't really discussed public displays of affection, but I find that I don't mind the modest show of how he feels, even if it does have his sister looking at the two of us like we're a pair of adorable puppies.

"Aww," she coos, snatching her yarn up and dumping it into her bag. "I'm going to go take my afternoon coffee break."

Carter lifts a brow at her. "Didn't you just take your lunch?"

Maya scoffs as she makes her way toward the

door. "Part-owner's prerogative." After sticking her tongue out at her brother like the mature twenty-something she is, she smiles at me and saunters out the door.

"Well, that wasn't at all obvious," Cater mutters. "But now that we're alone, I can do this." When Carter's soft lips brush against mine, all my thoughts melt away in favor of sinking into the bliss that is his kiss. For someone who proclaimed to need to practice dating, he sure as hell didn't need to practice this, or anything really. He just needed a confidence boost, and I am happy to have provided it. Carter pulls back and opens his mouth to say something, but the shop bell rings out again. "Did you forget something?" he asks, but when his eyes move toward the door, they widen as an apologetic look crosses his face.

My gaze follows his to find a beautiful, red-headed woman coming inside. She breezes past the display cases on her way over to the counter, her eyes lighting up when she sees Carter. Her red bow of a mouth turns up into a smile for him as she ignores me almost entirely. "Hello again." Her melodic voice rings out as she gives Carter an obvious once over. "I didn't forget anything, but it's been a while since I stopped in and thought I would see if you have anything I might be interested in. Remember me?"

Carter smiles politely and nods. "Um, it was Ms. Montgomery, right?" She nods and his eyes come together in thought. "Did you want to take a look around? Billie can guide you through the store if you'd like. She knows this place better than I do now." My chest squeezes with happiness at his words as well as the look of absolute pride on his face.

The woman ignores me and his question in favor of batting her eyelashes at him, leaning over the counter in a suggestive manner that would make a lot of men stand up and take notice, but not Carter. He only has eyes for me which is both a relief and a bit of a problem since technically we aren't even seeing each other and I'm supposed to be helping him get ready for the dating world, one that includes the woman that is practically throwing herself at him right now. "No. Today I'm just browsing, but I absolutely love the work you did on my stools. I can't stop admiring the craftsmanship." Her eyes flick to me dismissively for a moment before moving back to Carter. "Have you given any more thought to private lessons? I'm still very interested."

Woodworking lessons aren't what she's interested in, that much is obvious. Jealousy and possession rocket through me, and while I would love to reach up on my toes and kiss Carter, staking my claim for this woman to see, I know I have no right to do that. For his part, if Carter is affected at all by her glaring attempts to flirt with him, he doesn't show it. Instead, he moves closer to me and shakes his head at her. "Sorry, no. There are still too many safety issues involved."

The disinterest in his tone speaks to another reason why he's saying no, but the woman doesn't seem to pick up on it. Undeterred, the redhead presses on. "Well, maybe you could just talk to me about it over a cup of coffee or something instead." She ignores his brushing her off and leans further across the counter, her boobs practically spilling from her top, and I make a mental note to disinfect the surface the minute she leaves. "It could be fun."

Carter smiles tightly at her. "Thanks, but the shop keeps me pretty busy." He steps back toward the office. "Speaking of which, I should get back to work. Enjoy your browsing."

"Thanks," she calls. Her face is pinched as he

walks into the small office and shuts the door. With one last glance at me, the redhead marches from the shop without looking at another item.

Glaring at her back as she walks out, the moment the store is empty again, I spin on my heel and open the office door. Carter is inside, sitting on the chair with his hands clasped. "Is she gone?"

"Yes," I admit, though the jealousy I felt still lingers like a bad cough. "Why did you brush her off?" Even though it kills me to think so, he should be jumping at the chance to go out on dates now that he's more confident.

Carter frowns and stands from his seat. "What are you talking about?"

"She asked you out." I gesture towards the store and sigh. "What has all this practice been for if you don't accept offers for coffee from beautiful women who are obviously interested in you?"

His frown deepens, but he says nothing as he steps closer, his woodsy scent wafting over me and making me momentarily light-headed. Closing my eyes, I relish the feel of it, wondering if it might be for the last time. Maybe my prodding will have him rethinking his rejection of the buxom redhead and I'll be alone again. The thought makes me nauseated, but the feel of his calloused hands grabbing mine causes it to disappear. "Look at me, Billie." One eye squints open and he shakes my hands until I open both entirely. "Hear me when I say this. What we have been doing has never been just practice for me. *You* have never been just practice." He takes a deep breath and releases it slowly as his eyes bore into mine. "You're so much more than that." Swallowing the lump in my throat, I nod. It hasn't really felt like just practice to me either, but I'm not sure I'm ready to admit that yet. Carter's eyes narrow at me before he leans down and kisses my forehead. "I can see you still need some convincing."

"Carter—" I start, but stop when I don't know what to say.

He smiles and kisses my lips briefly before he walks toward the door. "I'm going back to work, but be prepared because I'm taking you out on a date tomorrow, Biliyana Kochev. A *very real* date."

With those parting words, he's out the door. As I'm left standing in the office like a dork with no idea what just occurred, two things happen. One, I have the feeling that things between the two of us just escalated and I'm going to need to figure my shit out sooner rather than later. And two, I can't stop smiling.

Chapter Twenty-One

Carter

It's been a couple of days since our talk in the shop, and while I was a little worried my confession might have scared Billie off, it hasn't. Every night we still end up in the same bed and yesterday she even closed the store for ten minutes and sneaked over to the workshop for a quickie, something I very much enjoyed but that now has me getting hard almost every time I look over at the workbench she bent over as she pulled me into her from behind. The sex has been more mind-blowing than I thought it would be, and I know that it's all because of Billie. Not only is she attentive to my needs and very responsive, but her being with me has given me the confidence to be more myself, in and out of the bedroom.

These days, I'm walking a little taller, laughing a lot more freely, and am generally a lot more pleasant to be around. Even some of the artisans we work with have remarked on it whenever they stop by, telling me that I look happier than they've ever seen me. It's because I am, and while I wasn't sure about telling Billie my feelings before, I'm sure about it now. Ever since my talk with Maya, I've thought about what she asked multiple times. Would I do a long distance relationship? *Absofuckinglutely.* It's only a three hour drive, and even though I only get one day off a week, I would happily spend it driving back and forth to see Billie if she really wanted to stay in Denver. And, if things progressed the way I would like them to, I would move there.

As much as I love the shop and want to honor my family by keeping it open, the more I thought about it, the more I knew my parents would want me to honor them by living the life I deserve, by falling in love and starting a family of my own. I'm in love with Billie, and as soon as she's ready, we can start a life together. Before it was easy to doubt whether or not she had feelings for me, too, but ever since our little talk in the shop, I know she does. I can *feel* it and I can see it in her eyes anytime we're together. What started off as just something to help me gain confidence quickly evolved into much more than that, and I'm not going to wait any longer to tell her.

Billie surprised me a few weeks ago with scented candles, lingerie, and the most amazing first time together. Tonight, I'm going to give her a surprise of my own to help convince her to give us a chance. I wanted to show Billie that even though I may have been helpless when it came to dating before, I'm not helpless when I'm with her. If anything, she makes me stronger than I think I ever have been, and I want her to see how well I can fit into her world, if that's what she wants from me. Dressed in my finest date night outfit of a dark green button down that Billie says brings out my eyes and a pair of brown slacks, I make my way into the shop carrying the dozen roses I purchased from the florist a few doors down.

Billie is in her usual late-summer uniform of a sleeveless jumpsuit, this one a light pink color that offsets her bronzed skin nicely. As much as I would like to skip to the end of the night where I can get my hands and mouth all over her, I want to treat her right and as she's meant to be treated, like the absolute marvel of a woman she is. When she finally turns to see me, her eyes widen and her mouth gapes open. "Wow. You look *really* good."

Stepping up to her, I hold the blooms to the side and lean down to brush a light kiss against her lips. "Thank you. You do, too." Presenting her with the flowers, I smile as she accepts them with a wide, pleased grin. "For you."

Billie dips her head near the rose buds and inhales. "They're beautiful," she tells me, hugging them to her chest. "You didn't have to get me flowers. I already have my favorite one next to my bed."

The wooden rose she's talking about has been next to her bed since the day I gifted it to her, and while nothing makes me happier than seeing her enjoy something I made especially for her, I also need her to know that I can be more than just a woodworker. "I wanted to get them for you." Leaning down to take a hit of the rose aroma, I sigh at the way they smell just like her. "They remind me of you. Besides, I was pretty sure that the wooden gifts would get old after a while, and I can't have you getting bored with me."

"I'll never get bored with you," she confesses instantly, smiling shyly as she walks over to the front door to lock up. When she's done, she gestures at my outfit and then the flowers. "Between the roses and the fantastic way you look tonight, I take it we're not just doing our usual Friday night pizza but are going on that date you promised me?"

Nodding my head, I lead her outside and to the passenger seat of my car. The small sedan isn't nearly as impressive as her sporty red car, but it's what I have and Billie has never minded it. In fact, she seems to prefer being the passenger to driving, even if it means being hauled around in my decade's old car. "Yes. I'm taking you out tonight. Somewhere nice."

Her eyes flick to her outfit and she gasps. "Am I dressed for it?" There are parts of her that seem so different than when I first met her, but her desire to always look her best and be dressed appropriately hasn't changed.

"You look beautiful," I tell her honestly. She's the

most beautiful person I have ever met, inside and out, and after tonight, she'll know exactly how I feel about her. I lean down and give her a quick peck on the cheek before helping her into the car. Once I'm in the driver's seat, I look over at Billie, watching her admire the flowers for another moment before resting them on her lap. "Buckle up. We've got a bit of a drive."

She raises a brow in question, and when I don't answer she does exactly what I asked and secures herself. "That's fine as long as I get to be DJ the whole time." Before I can agree, she already has the radio on and is searching through stations. We're almost to the highway by the time she settles on a pop station. "You really need to invest in satellite radio, my friend. There is a dance station that plays all the best numbers to move to."

Tossing a wry smile her way, I steer us onto the road that leads to Green Valley. "Call me crazy, but the last thing I think about while I'm driving is dancing."

"Have it your way," she says, her body swaying. She looks so good doing it that I have a hard time keeping my eyes on the road. "More dancing for me."

"I think we both know you're the one that looks good doing it anyway." The more she moves, the more my desire to turn around and head straight home ramps up, but I steel my resolve, white knuckling the wheel to keep my blood from rushing south. She does look really good dancing, and even though I look like a man throwing his back out whenever I attempt it, I can't wait until she sees the surprise I have in store for her tonight.

As our journey continues, we chat and laugh a lot, sharing stories from our days and some from our pasts. Billie talks about some of the wilder things she did in her youth, and I blush when she admits to skinny dipping in a swimming pool at college with some of her girlfriends. Luckily, I'm saved from her sharing any more memories that have my pants tightening when I steer onto the Green Valley exit and Billie takes in the sights.

"This place is so cute," she remarks. The town is slightly larger than Starlight Lake thanks to the ski resort that's located about twenty minutes further into the mountains. The lodge is a nice place and somewhere I would love to take Billie, but tonight we're headed somewhere else. We drive down the main drag, finally pulling over into a parking lot that's tucked away to the side of the major street. When I park, Billie looks out the window and then at me, her eyes wide. "This is where we're going?"

Nodding, I step outside and round the car to her door. When she slips her hand in mine, she looks happy, but there is a reluctance on her face I didn't expect to see. "Is this not somewhere you want to go?"

Billie shakes her head, a small smile on her face. "It looks beautiful," she confesses. The Italian restaurant is a red brick building with a front patio lit up by hundreds of twinkle lights. The best part is inside where they have live music and dancing on Friday and Saturday nights. I made the reservation last week, hoping she would love it, but maybe I was wrong. "It's just that I don't need anything fancy."

Narrowing my eyes, I loop her arm through mine and start toward the front door. "Are you sure about that, Miss Egyptian cotton bedsheets?"

Billie smiles at the comment, but pulls me to the side of the walkway. "There is a difference between *liking* nice things and *needing* them." Her eyes search mine as she cups my face. "This is wonderful. I just wanted you to know that I don't need it to have a good time with you."

Nodding, I lean down and kiss her lips. "Maybe I need to show you that I can do nice things for you."

Tugging her arm, I start walking again. "Will you let me do this for you?"

Billie mock sighs and gives me a withering look. "If I have to," she grumbles before bouncing on her heels and leading us up and into the restaurant. As she takes in the deep burgundy walls and dark wood floors, her expression looks pleased, but it becomes absolutely joyful when she sees the band in the corner and a few couples already enjoying a dance. "Dancing?" When I nod, she hugs me tighter than she ever has and kisses me on the cheek. "Best date ever."

My heart swells at the exclamation and after giving my name to the hostess, we're seated near the dancefloor. After two courses of stuffed mushrooms and pesto gnocchi, we sit back contentedly in our seats and stare at one another. Billie's eyes flick to the dancefloor, and I don't have to think twice about my next move. Standing, I go to her chair and offer my hand. "May I have this dance?"

Billie beams up at me and takes my hand, the zing of excitement I feel expected now since it happens every time we touch. "You can have all my dances". A shadow crosses over her face for the briefest of moments, but it's gone before I can decipher what it is.

When we reach the square of flooring sectioned off for dancing, I pull her in my arms as the band plays some song that sounds vaguely Italian but I can't identify. All that matters to me is that the song has a slow tempo so that I don't end up making a fool of myself. As we sway to the music, Billie leans her head against my shoulder, humming contentedly along with the melody of the song. One slow song bleeds into another as we continue to dance. With Billie secured in my arms, everything is right in the world and nothing else matters. The music, the other people, even the restaurant itself fades into the background as all of my focus rests on the woman pressed against me. I've never been in love before, but even if I had known what it felt like already, that past love wouldn't hold a candle to what I'm feeling now. A warm glow fills my chest as I think about a future with Billie, a future that can only happen if I tell her how I feel. As I bask in the feeling of loving her, time passes in a haze, and when the band starts playing a faster song, it could have been minutes or hours since we first stepped out onto the floor.

Pulling her gaze up to mine, I stare into Billie's brown eyes. Nothing feels as right as she does, no one will ever compare to her, and I need to tell her. "Billie."

"Yes?" Her breath is feathery and light, like it could float away on the slightest of breezes, but I want to do everything I can in my power to keep everything about her right here with me, forever.

My eyes bore into hers, hoping to convey just how much I feel for her before I can say it. "I love you," I confess. My voice is steady, never wavering because I have never been more certain of anything in my entire life.

"Carter," she starts, her eyes widening at my words. She looks happy, but that happiness soon morphs into confusion. The old Carter would have seen that and balked, been too polite or too hurt to push forward, but the new me knows better. The confusion I see isn't about us, but about her. For all her confidence, Billie still has that doubt that she's nothing more than a pretty face, and while her face is beyond beautiful, she has so much more to offer than that. Clearly she needs to hear it again, so I quickly pull her outside to the small garden the restaurant uses to grow its own vegetables to tell her as much.

Turning to her, I cup her face, my heart swelling when she closes her eyes and automatically leans into the touch. "Billie, I love you." Her eyes blink open and I see so many conflicting emotions playing there. "Maybe this wasn't the best place or time for me to say it, but I needed you to hear it. And it's okay if you aren't there yet or aren't ready to say it back because I don't need to hear the words. I just need you."

Billie's eyes go glassy and I catch a tear that falls with my thumb. "But I don't know what I'm doing. What if I find a job back in Denver? Or somewhere else?" She sniffles, so I pull her against my chest and lean my head against hers, inhaling the scent of roses to help calm myself and find the words to help comfort her.

"Then I will go with you." She gasps lightly and pulls back to look at me, and I smile at her. "I can do what I do from anywhere, and, yeah, it might be a little harder than doing it in Starlight Lake where I have a shop all set up, but I don't care. You're worth the extra effort." She starts to dispute me, but I kiss her instead. It tastes salty from her tears, but I can feel her putting the love she has for me into it, even if she isn't ready to say the words yet. When I pull back, Billie nods at me, her expression thoughtful and slightly perplexed. "I can see that you need a bit of time with this, and that is something I can easily give you," I tell her as I lead us toward the door. Spinning around, I hold her face in my hands and gaze at her, trying to express the seriousness of my words. "But I want you to know that no matter what you decide you want to do or where you want to live, I just need you. You are enough just as you are now, and I will tell you that every single day for the rest of my life if you'll let me."

Wide-eyed, Billie nods, but I see the corners of her mouth twitch with the need to smile. As I lead us back inside and to our table, I come up with a plan to help her see just how amazing she is, and just how much I love her.

Chapter Twenty-Two

Billie

Every morning for the last week, Carter has woken me up with a kiss, like some kind of fairy tale Prince Charming, and whispered the same seven words to me as I blink myself awake. "I love you and you are enough." Each time he says it, a bit of the doubt I have about that statement gets chipped away, and I spend the rest of my day lighter on my feet and with a bit of the weight I've been carrying about the future off my chest. The fact that he also says those same words before we go to sleep every night helps too. Sometimes they're spoken as we lay in bed, cuddling under his new flannel blanket as he talks about all of the plans he has for the two of us, and sometimes they're whispered in my ear before he slides between my legs and makes love to me until I'm coming apart with pleasure as well as the inability to contain all the love he has for me and I for him. And I do love him.

Loving Carter is easy, it's admitting to myself that I'm ready for and worthy of his love that has been difficult. He has had no such qualms, telling me over and over again how much he cares for me while also letting me know that he doesn't care if I figure out what I want to do for a job now, ten years from now, or never. They're words that I need to hear because somewhere along the way, I assumed that I had to have a career path, have something to offer beyond my looks in order to be worthy of someone like him, someone responsible, caring, and thoughtful when all along, I was all of those things too. It was just hard to see that when I've been a little too caught up in my own bullshit insecurities. I helped Carter see his worth, how he could be *wanted* in addition to how much we all need him. He's been trying to show me how much he wants and *needs* me, I just wasn't ready to see it before, but I am now. Before I tell him that, there are two things I need to mark off my to-do list.

As I sit on the stairs up to our apartment, a smile comes over my face as I think about the look on Maya's face when I asked her to cover my shift today because I had important things to do. At first she looked surprised, but after scanning my face for a second, she grinned and nodded. "Do what you need to do to be happy," she told me, and so I am.

The call to my parents finally connects and I smile at the loudness of my father's voice. "Biliyana," he exclaims. His voice is something I've missed hearing every day when I would pop by and see him in his office, but now that I've been going without those daily visits, I can hear just how happy he is and probably always has been to speak with me. I never noticed it before, instead always worried about hearing disappointment in his voice. But not anymore. "How is life in the mountains? Have you seen any bears yet?"

The faint sound of my mom's voice comes over the speaker as she scolds him in Bulgarian about not being allowed to box with a bear and I chuckle. My dad is a bear of a man himself, and while I wouldn't put it past him to try and fight one of the ferocious animals, I wouldn't put money on him winning that particular battle either. "I agree with Mom. No picking fights with bears when you come to visit."

"We're allowed to come visit now?" my father asks. He mentioned wanting to see me but also wanting to give me space to do my own thing, so I told them they could come when I had everything all figured out. That still hasn't happened, but I'm done waiting for that part of my life to come together because being with Carter is more important than having all of my so-called ducks in a row. My heart and my head knows what it wants as far as he is concerned. Everything else will come with time, and if not, that's okay too. "Does that mean you have found your light?"

"Well, I guess that depends on how you meant that," I tell him. "I'm still not sure what I want to do for a career, but for now I'm having a great time working at the shop and spending time with Carter."

Shuffling noises muffle the speaker and I hear my mom's voice louder than ever now. "You and this young man are dating, yes?" she asks. I can hear the hopefulness in her voice and luckily I get to confirm her suspicions.

"We are," I confess. We are a lot more than that, but Carter gets to hear that before my parents do. "He's really special and I can't wait for you to meet him."

"This is wonderful news," my mom exclaims before her voice disappears. I can already picture her running down the hallway of their house to grab the landline and call all her friends to spread the word that I am *finally* off the market.

"Okay then," I chuckle before my dad picks up his phone again. He sniffles on the other end of the line and I worry that maybe my news wasn't as exciting to him as it was to my mom. Is he disappointed in my lack of direction professionally? He was always so driven that it wouldn't surprise me. "Are you okay, Dad?"

"Yes," he says through a watery laugh. "I am just so happy to hear you happy, Biliyana. You haven't sounded like this since you were a young woman and it makes me proud to know that you've found something that lights you up."

Suddenly feeling a bit emotional myself, I wipe a rogue tear from my eye and swallow thickly. "And you're okay with it being a person and not a job?"

He huffs a breath. "It never had to be a job, and as long as this Carter person treats you well and loves you as you deserve, I am more than okay with it. In fact, I am going to get our jet prepped for a visit this weekend."

My eyes widen at the thought of my parents descending on the two of us that quickly. "I'm sure he'll be excited to meet you, but maybe let me clear that with Carter first."

"Well, what are you waiting for? Go do that because I want to meet the man that has captured my daughter's heart." After a quick goodbye, I end the call and smile down at my phone. If I had bothered to talk to my parents about all of this sooner, I might have been able to avoid the doubts that have plagued my mind since leaving Denver, but even so, I'm not mad at how things have turned out because they brought me to where I am now—in love with an amazing guy who loves me for me, someone he sees as equally as incredible as he is. With one important conversation down, I shoot off a text and prepare myself for the next one.

Ten minutes later, Jake appears at the end of the alley, nodding at me as he comes closer. He's dressed for work and even though his office space is just a short walk away from Hodgepodge and I could have gone to him, I wanted to do this somewhere I felt comfortable. The shop and the apartment I share with Carter has become a source of comfort for me, and I need to draw on that as I confront my best friend. From the look of trepidation on his face, Jake knows he's in trouble, I'm just not sure he knows why. He warned me away from Carter so often, making me doubt my own intentions, and while my reticence at telling Carter I love him wasn't exactly Jake's fault, his comments didn't help either. When he gets a few steps below me, his expression turns contrite and he holds up his hands. "Before you start, can I say something?"

"Sure," I tell him. My arms cross over my chest as I stare at him. Angry isn't the word I would use to describe my feelings, but sad definitely fits the bill. I may have played up my party girl persona, but he's supposed to know me better than that and the fact that he wasn't very supportive of me stings more than a little bit.

Jake exhales slowly as he takes the seat next to me. "I know that I've been a bad friend," he starts. Jake has always been good about knowing and admitting his faults, but I didn't expect this. Hiding my shock is difficult, but I manage to do it as he goes on. "You've been going through a lot, and I haven't made the time to really help you deal with any of that. The years I was in Denver and missing Maya like crazy, you were always there for me and I feel like an asshole for not returning the favor."

With a sigh, I turn to him. "Jake, you have a kid and a fiancée. I didn't really expect us to be hanging out all the time. Besides, I had someone else to keep me company and help me deal with things."

Jake nods, his auburn curls bouncing slightly. "I know, and that's the other thing I'm sorry about." He brushes his hands down his slacks and smiles sadly. "I shouldn't have interfered with anything that was happening between you and Carter. I was just so happy to finally have Maya and JJ in my life that I didn't want anything to mess that up. But I should have known you better, known that even if you hadn't wanted anything serious with him, you never would have treated him poorly. You're not like that, and I'm really sorry that I let myself forget it."

My head bobs as I exhale all my pent up frustration and sadness at him. "Wow," I breathe out, giving him a once over Narrowing my eyes at him, I bump his shoulder with mine. "I didn't expect you to admit all that and I'm a little irritated that I don't get to yell at you now."

Jake huffs a laugh and bumps me right back. "You can still yell at me if you want to."

"Meh," I say with a shrug. "It's not as fun if I have your permission." Even though he's just taken the wind out of my sails, I'm not upset about it. If anything, I'm glad I didn't have a blow-out with my best friend.

"Fair enough," Jake adds, his smile looking less strained. "So, you love him, huh?"

Nodding, I gaze over at the workshop where I know Carter is hard at work on something incredible. No matter what he's making it will be as awesome and awe-inspiring as he is. "I really do," I admit. Pulling myself up, I turn and offer a hand to Jake and smile when he takes it. "I should probably go tell him that."

Jake chuckles as we walk down the steps together. "Probably," he agrees, pulling me into a hug. "But if you have the same look on your face when you're with him as you do right now, I think he already knows." Winking, Jake pulls back and walks away, disappearing into the alley.

Maybe Carter does already know that I love him, but he still deserves to hear it. Walking into the workshop, I smile when I see Carter carving symbols and figures onto the front of a door. With each piece he makes, he gets better and better and I have no doubt that soon he's going to be even more in-demand than he is now. As long as he comes home to me at the end of the day, I'm more than happy for him. His lips purse as he blows across the surface of the wood, flecks of sawdust taking flight as he does. Since he's using hand tools, I feel confident that I can interrupt him without getting another safety lecture, not that I'd mind one. Stern Carter is just as sexy as all the others, and I'm excited to get to spend my days and nights telling him that.

"Hey, you," I call out as I make my approach.

His eyes meet mine and a smile spreads across his face. Putting his tools down and dusting off his hands, he reaches out and pulls me into his chest. "Hey," he says, kissing me briefly. "This is a nice surprise. I thought you were taking the day off."

"I am. I just had to come and tell you something." Wrapping my arms a little tighter around him, I smile and try to convey how I'm feeling without words.

Carter clocks my expression and his eyes fill with hope. "Yeah?" he asks, his voice low and thick.

"Yeah." Nodding, I raise up on my toes and kiss him deeply, with as much passion and love as I can pouring out of me and over to him. When we part, he looks slightly dazed and I feather my lips against his one last time. "I just wanted to tell you that I love you, and you are enough."

Carter's breath hitches and his eyes shine with happiness. "I love you, too, and thank you, *Elskling.*" He draws me into his chest for another hug and rests his head against mine. "Thank you for loving me, thinking that I am enough, and knowing that you are too."

A contented sigh escapes me as we hold one another. "Sorry it took me so long to figure it out."

"Don't be," he says, kissing the top of my head. "I would have waited forever for you."

Smiling, I turn and look deeply into his eyes. "I'm glad you didn't have to." As he leans down and captures my lips with his once again, I'm grateful for his patience and for my own. I may not have everything figured out, but what I do have is everything I want and everything I need right here in my arms. And that's enough.

Epilogue

Carter
Three Months Later

Twinkle lights sparkle overhead in the town square as couples sway and dance to music provided by The Big Band, the aptly named group of musicians playing swing-style music like the kind that was popular nearly one hundred years ago. Right now a lively tune plays as a number of invited party guests and some onlookers from all over town and beyond dance and spin all over the cobblestone of the square. Jake and Maya's wedding was supposed to be a small affair, but it turns out when you live and work in a small town, everyone within earshot of your wedding announcement wants to help you celebrate. And when the ceremony is held in a public place, well, it can become a bit of a spectacle. From the look of utter joy on my sister's and her now-husband's faces, they either haven't noticed or don't care. When you're as in love with someone as they are with each other and you're in one another's arms, nothing else matters.

That is certainly what it's been like for me over the last few months. After Billie came into my workshop and told me she loved me, everything that didn't concern the two of us or our happiness just kind of melted away. We combined our bedrooms and created a guest room for JJ that doubles as an office for Billie. Sometimes she goes in there to explore what other possible careers she might be interested in, but more often than not she ends up spending her time on the computer to scout out new artisans to feature in the store. She seems to really be at home at Hodgepodge, and even if that only lasts a while longer, I'm glad she's happy and has figured out that she doesn't need to have a career or a professional direction in life for me to want her, to need her. As long as she is okay with me tagging along for the ride, I am happy to go anywhere she wants.

Glancing over at the beautiful woman next to me, I smile as I lift our intertwined fingers to kiss the back of her hand. Noticing the increased chill in the air despite the whole area being packed with portable heaters, I grab the faux fur shawl that goes with her "Best Woman" dress and drape it across her shoulders. "Enjoying the salad, *Elskling*?" I ask, nodding at her nearly full plate.

Billie prods the ranch covered lettuce with her fork before turning to me with a dubious expression on her face. "I know Jake tried this salad and it rocked his world or whatever, but I don't get it," she admits. Shrugging, she grabs the champagne flute filled with sparkling apple cider and takes a sip. "I guess I'm still a bit of a food snob."

My chuckle causes a little puff of smoke to appear in front of us, but despite the cold weather, I feel warm all over just like I do any time I am in Billie's presence. "The Hot Pocket you demolished last night while we watched trash television speaks to the contrary."

Billie shakes her head as she deposits her glass back on the linen-topped table in front of us. We're at a table with the couple of the hour, Jake and Billie's parents, and JJ. "*Love Boat: Deserted Island Edition* is not trash. It's peak TV and I will die on this hill." She turns to her father who sits in the seat next to her. "Right, Dad?"

Ivan nods his silver covered head and winks at his daughter. "Absolutely, Biliyana. Your mother and I can't get enough of the show the two of you introduced us to last time we were here."

Billie's parents came to visit her not one week

after she told me she loved me. When I met the two of them, her mom walked up and kissed both of my cheeks, her eyes shining with happiness. Her dad looked far more reserved, stern even, and when I held my hand out to shake, the man gripped it in his own meaty paw before pulling me into a giant bear hug, telling me he was happy to finally have a son. Billie looked embarrassed by their over-the-top display, but after so many years of not having parents of my own, I relished the attention and we spent most of their visit bonding over mutual interests, including group watching a certain reality show. Eventually I did have to draw the line at us going searching for bears in the woods, something Billie assured me was nothing but a joke, but her dad looked so downtrodden when we didn't go that I have my doubts.

The band stops playing and everyone in the square claps, including JJ who has spent most of the evening between Billie's and Jake's mothers who have been plying him with fish-shaped crackers to keep him calm and behaved. Between the two of them, he'll be so stuffed full of carbs that he'll probably fall asleep before his parents get a chance to cut the cake. After a deep breath, I lean over and kiss Billie on the cheek. "That's my cue," I tell her.

"Good luck," she says with a smile.

Billie's Best Woman speech was fantastic. It was funny, emotional, and really spoke to how much she knew Jake and how happy he has been since coming back to my sister. My speech will be a little different. When I told Maya about my idea, she squealed happily and clapped, insisting that I go through with it. As I make my way up to the stage where the band is set up and grab the microphone from the lead singer, I swallow down the last of my nerves and toss up a silent prayer to my parents for courage.

Clearing my throat off mic, I smile and greet the crowd. "Good evening. For those of you who don't know me, I am Maya's brother and Man of Honor, and it is my privilege to be up here to wish her and Jake all the happiness that they deserve." People clap at this and I wait for it to die down before I continue. "You may not know their story and I won't share it now, though, boy, is it a doozy." A few laughs erupt and I smile at my sister who shakes her head at me lovingly. "Things weren't always easy for the two of them, but their love for one another never wavered, and it's that kind of love that I think we all strive for, the kind of love the world could use a little more of."

Signaling to the band leader, I watch as they gather their instruments and prepare to play the song we agreed on weeks ago. "Anyone who knows Maya knows that she's a romantic, and so it is with her full permission and insistence that I try to bring a little more of that kind of love here tonight." Nodding to the band behind me and patting the pocket of my tux jacket to make sure I still have the ring, I spin back to the front and listen as they start to play the opening notes of Bruno Mars's *I Think I Want to Marry You*. Maya squeals and whips her head over at Billie who is staring at me wide-eyed, her mouth dropped open in surprise before it starts to pull into a wide grin.

Jumping off the stage, I start to sing the lyrics I know by heart, and even if I didn't, it wouldn't be hard for me to conjure them up when they talk about wanting to marry the person you love. A big proposal like this is risky, but between the number of times we've laid together in bed and discussed our future and her moving all of her stuff from storage in Denver to our apartment, I feel confident enough in her answer. Her telling me she loves me multiple times per day helps too. As I dance between tables, out of the corner of my eye I can see people swaying in their chairs and others dancing near the street, but my eyes never leave those of the woman I love. Finally, I make it over to her and drop down to one knee just as the last line leaves my mouth. When the song ends, applause erupts, but I barely hear it. All I can concentrate on is the woman in front of me whose brown eyes are filled with a beautiful mix of exhilaration and contentment.

Turning off the mic and placing it on the table, I pull the ring out of my pocket and present it to her. Her eyes widen when she spies the ring I was able to get from her mom. The gold antique band with intricate carving belonged to her grandmother and will look beautiful on her finger, if she says yes. "What do you say, *Elskling*? Will you marry me?"

Billie looks at me, her eyes shining in the twinkle lights and her expression one of utter bliss. "I will absolutely marry you, Viking." After slipping the ring on her finger, I whoop loudly and jump to my feet, pulling her to standing and straight into my arms. The crowd roars their approval as I sway with the love of my life in my arms.

When I pull back, I see her chuckling and shaking her head at me. "What are you laughing about?" I ask, unable to wipe the smile off my face.

"That damned fountain really is magic," she says. Grinning like a couple of fools in love, we kiss deeply, public display be damned.

When we pull back, I rest our foreheads together and smile at my fiancée. "You're magic." Maybe my wish from years ago finally came true or maybe circumstances just brought me the person that makes my life complete. Regardless of how she came to me, I'm grateful she did, and I look forward to a future with Billie that may not always be as magical as it is tonight, but no matter what we face, we'll do it together. I can't think of anything more perfect than that.

The End

EVERNIGHT PUBLISHING ®

www.evernightpublishing.com